The Interplanetary Relations Bureau had one basic rule: 'Democracy imposed from without is the severest form of tyrany.' That was why the IPR teams working throughout the galaxy operated in secret, mingling with the unsuspecting natives in their efforts to bring democracy to the humanoid worlds.

Kurr, though, was a problem: the King's shrewd understanding of his down-trodden people, backed up with periodic torture, defeated the IPR's efforts. Until Cultural Survey Officer Forzon arrived. Despite a frightening lack of knowledge, a price on his head and treason in his own ranks, Forzon fought his own unorthodox way to a solution that resulted in a revolution.

The Still, Small Voice of Trumpets

LLOYD BIGGLE Jr

SPHERE BOOKS LIMITED
30/32 Gray's Inn Road, London WC1X 8JL

First published in Great Britain by Rapp and Whiting Ltd 1969
Copyright © Lloyd Biggle Jr 1968
Copyright © The Condé Nast Publication Inc 1961

This novel is based on a short story which appeared in
Analog magazine

TRADE
MARK

Set in Linotype Times

Printed in Great Britain by
Hazell Watson & Viney Ltd
Aylesbury, Bucks

ONE

Behind him a door opened and closed. Jef Forzon kept his attention on the paintings that filled one wall of the room from floor to ceiling.

Magnificent paintings.

The first thing he would do, he thought, would be to put a chemist to work on that paint. He'd never seen anything like it. The colors were superb, the texture astonishing. In the hands of the better artists, and most of those represented in the display were better artists, it produced an effect of dimension that made his head spin.

Small wonder that the Interplanetary Relations Bureau had sent a distress call for a Cultural Survey officer! Personnel who botched the simple task of lettering door signs and selected office color schemes more suitable to a darkened mausoleum were ill-equipped to cope with works of art. They didn't even know how to hang a painting!

The room's communicator sputtered; the receptionist said coldly, 'The coordinator will see you now, sir.'

Forzon got to his feet, paused for one last, searching look at the paintings, and followed her. He loved his work, but he hated the bureaucratic formalities that had to be negotiated en route to it. He also hated shapely young ladies who wore masculine uniforms and smiled superior smiles.

This particular young lady's smile vanished abruptly, and Forzon realized, with a twinge of conscience, that he had been glaring at her. He owed her an apology. The superior smile could have been the only one she had, and the uniform probably was not of her own choosing, or at least he hoped that it wasn't.

'Do the base personnel ever wear native costume?' he asked.

5

'Sir?'

The thought so startled her that a door slipped from her fingers and slammed in Forzon's face. She opened it again, and he followed her along a corridor reading the signs on the doors that he passed: *Team A Headquarters, Team B Headquarters*, and then an unlabeled room that was perhaps destined to become his own Cultural Survey Headquarters, in which case he would paint the sign himself. He had never worked under the direct control of another governmental agency, and with each step that brought him closer to the coordinator he liked the idea less.

'There's no rule against it, is there?' he asked the girl.

'Sir?'

'Wearing native costume,' Forzon persisted, regarding her near-masculine hair styling with sturdy masculine disapproval. 'There's no rule against it, is there?'

'No, sir. But the coordinator does not approve.'

Forzon's resentment for this particular coordinator was rapidly changing to active dislike. He couldn't blame the man for not getting up in the middle of the night to check him in when he arrived, but there was no excuse for his keeping Forzon waiting for more than an hour the following morning – not that he had minded, with the paintings to study, but he knew that it was unnecessary.

Deliberate rudeness on the part of a planet's ranking officer was difficult enough to cope with; rudeness combined with a proclivity for petty tyranny would be intolerable. In most headquarters the personnel delighted in wearing native costume.

But it was no business of his. He would complete the formalities as quickly as possible and get out among the natives where he belonged.

The receptionist saw him through another door, gave him a pert nod, and left him. Another young lady, equally severe in appearance, passed him along to a private office. Forzon strolled calmly into the presence of Wern Rastadt,

6

Interplanetary Relations Bureau coordinator of the planet Gurnil.

'Forzon reporting,' he said.

The words brought no discernible pleasure to the face of Coordinator Rastadt. Flabby, deeply wrinkled with a morosely drooping mouth, it was not a face capable of expressing pleasure. The eyes, for all their blazing aliveness, were sunken in unhealthy puffs of flesh. A tonsorist had valiantly attempted to impose a stiff military cut upon the sparse white hair and succeeded only in exposing a vast expanse of pink scalp. Only the coordinator's chin had character: it jutted firmly, like an incongruous prominence in a dreary wasteland. His plump white hands were held palm down on the desk in front of him, as though he were tensing himself to spring at Forzon.

Obviously he had grown old and fat in the service, waived voluntary retirement, and entrenched himself in a soft assignment from which, barring a colossal blunder and a special competency investigation, only death would him part. Forzon turned his gaze to the framed motto attached to the wall behind the coordinator – DEMOCRACY IMPOSED FROM WITHOUT IS THE SEVEREST FORM OF TYRANNY – and suppressed a smile. It was the fifth time that morning that he had encountered it.

Abruptly Rastadt's hands folded into fists, and his words lashed at Forzon. 'I don't suppose the Cultural Survey teaches its men how to report to a superior officer!'

Forzon said easily, 'Superiority is a myth. The Cultural Survey proved that long ago.'

Rastadt's fists hit the desk. He jerked erect, his chair overturned and crashed to the floor, and he leaned across the desk and shouted, 'You are now a part of my command, and by God, you're going to conduct yourself as if you knew it. Get outside and come back in here and report properly!'

Forzon reluctantly thrust aside the temptation to have some fun with this obnoxious martinet. The man's age and

7

position entitled him to a certain rudimentary respect, even if his conduct did not. Forzon tossed his credentials onto the desk. The coordinator studied them silently.

When finally he spoke his voice sounded curiously subdued. 'You're a – a *sector supervisor* – in the Cultural Survey?'

'So I've been told.'

The coordinator turned, carefully righted his chair, and sat down heavily. Forzon had never seen a man so quickly and so thoroughly deflated. He gazed unblinkingly at Forzon, his flabby face suddenly tense with incredulity.

Watching him, Forzon detachedly weighed the pictorial qualities of his bloated features and found them wanting. A portrait painter who had to wrest character from that bleak visage would be driven to distraction. On the other hand, a caricaturist could have had a delightful time with it.

'You're young,' Rastadt observed suddenly.

'That happens once to everyone.'

'May I have your orders, please.'

'I was told that my orders would be waiting for me here.'

'Here?' Rastadt's head jerked, and the puffy flesh contracted and made suspicious slits of his eyes. 'I have no orders for you.' He paused. 'Then you don't know why you're here?'

'Why am I anywhere? To set up a cultural survey.'

'No.' The coordinator shook his head emphatically. 'No. Gurnil is still classified a hostile planet. Cultural surveys are not permitted on hostile planets, as you should know.'

'My headquarters ordered me to this planet,' Forzon said slowly. 'The Interplanetary Relations Bureau cleared the orders, gave me a class one priority, and even arranged to have a cruiser go a number of light years out of its way to deposit me on your doorstep. Are you trying to tell me that I'm lost?'

Rastadt pushed Forzon's credentials toward him. 'The only information I've received was a short message informing me that a CS man had been transferred to the Bureau *in rank* for service on this planet. The message didn't say what the rank was or what the service was to be, but I'm certain that it can't have anything to do with a cultural survey. You're no longer a CS man, you're IPR or you wouldn't be here. It's odd that you don't have orders, though.'

'It's odder that my orders haven't arrived.'

'Not really. We're due for a supply contact, and no doubt they'll be in the regular mail. You got here ahead of them because you came by cruiser. Normally the IPR Bureau furnishes a copy of orders for presentation when reporting for duty, but in your case, since you're transferring from another service, I suppose there was a mixup.' He turned away and absently spoke to the far wall. 'Whatever your assignment is, you'll need briefing.'

'No,' Forzon said, speaking with considerably more calmness than he felt, 'but you will. Do IPR officers customarily regard their superiors as a pack of ignoramuses? No one but an idiot would handpick a man who is a highly trained specialist in one small area of a complicated field of knowledge and then assign him to doing something else. Your superiors aren't, and they haven't. Surely the IPR Bureau wouldn't be requisitioning a Cultural Survey officer if it didn't have a job that only a man with his training could handle.'

'I'm sure that when your orders come—'

'I don't need orders to tell me what my job is.' Forzon seated himself familiarly on a corner of the coordinator's desk and pointed a finger. 'You have a number of native paintings in your reception room. They're splendid works of art, and some nincompoop has attached them to the wall with *cellex*, which for all practical purposes makes them part of the building. If I find out who did it I may murder him. One of the paintings is a portrait of a musician. Do you know which one I mean?'

'I seem to recall—'

'Good. The musical instrument is a plucked chordo-

9

phone, which for the want of a better term I'm calling a harp – though it's totally unlike any harp I've even seen or heard of. It has a beautifully carved frame, and the strings are stretched from the perimeter of a globular sounding medium to converge in a sort of dragon's head that ornaments the top of the instrument.' He paused. The coordinator was gaping at him wide-eyed. 'What I want to know is this: what musical scale does that instrument employ?'

'I'm—' The coordinator's throat bulged as he tried to swallow. 'I'm afraid I don't know.'

'I was afraid you wouldn't. Would you send a selection of recordings up to my quarters, along with the equipment to play them?'

'*Recordings?*'

'Of the instrument's music. You do have some, don't you?'

'I'm – I'm afraid not.'

'I see. Then I'll make my own. Can you round up the equipment and a few musicians to play for me, or do I have to do that myself?'

'But that's—' The coordinator's voice cracked.

'Nothing,' Forzon announced with deadly calm, 'is impossible. These paintings interest me. I want the chemical analysis of the paint and a few of the colors to experiment with.'

The coordinator had lapsed into speechlessness. 'No chemical analysis?' Forzon asked resignedly.

'Not that I know of.'

'It shouldn't be difficult to make one. You do maintain a laboratory here, don't you? Give me a little of the paint, and I'll analyze it myself.'

'I'm afraid—'

'No laboratory?'

'No paint.'

'That shouldn't be much of a problem. Get some. Better – invite a few artists in. I'd like to see them work.'

'But that's impossible! You see—'

'I see why someone has seen fit to send you a Cultural Survey officer.'

The coordinator's face had reddened; his rising blood pressure seemed on collision course with his plunging self-control, but when finally he spoke his tone was that of a man with a grievance. 'You don't see at all. There isn't much we can do until your orders arrive, but I'll tell my assistant to brief you. Are your quarters satisfactory? Well, then – good morning, Forzon. *Supervisor* Forzon, I should say.'

He scrambled to his feet and snapped off a salute. Forzon returned it dumbfoundedly and withdrew from the office with the disconcerting feeling that he'd been routed.

He made his way back to the reception room and seated himself to have another look at the paintings. He *had* to have an analysis of that paint. He had to make some recordings. The mere sight of that strange instrument evoked dazzling phantasms of rippling sound.

The receptionist was regarding him with hostility, as though she suspected him of harboring one of the more loathsome species of native vermin. He said conversationally, 'I don't suppose you know what sort of a musical scale that instrument employs.'

Her hostility vanished. For a distressing moment what had been a rather attractive face became suffused with a thoroughly unattractive, blank astonishment. She did not answer, and Forzon, who found unattractive things repulsive, turned away.

Beauty he loved for its own sake; ugliness, which more often than not was a form of inverted beauty, fascinated him. Life offered far too little of either, and far too much appalling mediocrity, which he thought hideous.

But this world of Gurnil possessed a cultural complex of well-nigh unbelievable richness. The paintings contained tantalizing evidence of other arts that might equal or surpass them: the musical instrument; its masterfully sculpted frame that proclaimed a high level of craftsmanship in the

11

plastic arts; the striking architecture, houses with walls that flared outward from a narrow base, and with their humped roofs and splendid colors looked like brilliant, rectangular mushrooms. If what followed was anything on the order of this dazzling introduction, the planet Gurnil had to be the kind of world every Cultural Survey officer dreamed about but almost never encountered.

Forzon's elation was tempered by a strong sense of foreboding. The IPR Bureau could have contracted as much cultural survey as it needed without transferring a high-ranking CS official to the Bureau in rank; and having requisitioned such an officer, it would not send his orders by slow freighter.

The receptionist continued to regard him with hostility. He looked at her inquiringly; she scowled back at him. He stole another glance at the shimmering portrait of a magnificently feminine young lady of Gurnil, who wore her hair in long, luxurious tresses and whose lustrous robes and abundance of frills concealed her shapeliness without distorting it.

The shoulders of the receptionist's uniform jacket had been padded into a rigid angularity, and any competent designer of women's apparel should have known better than to disfigure a natural curvilinear beauty with sharp angles. The half-length trousers were, if possible, a worse mistake. Their color reminded Forzon of congealed mud, and beside it the healthy flesh of even the most shapely legs took on a corpse-like pallor.

The contrast was so stark and unsettling that Forzon abandoned the paintings forthwith and marched off to his quarters where he could pick this puzzle apart in private. He had a disquieting feeling of certitude that when he succeeded, when he finally found out what was happening on the planet Gurnil – he wouldn't like it.

TWO

The walls of Forzon's two small, sparsely furnished rooms were dismal expanses of faded gray plastic, their only ornaments the black-framed IPR motto displayed in each room: *DEMOCRACY IMPOSED FROM WITHOUT IS THE SEVEREST FORM OF TYRANNY.*

His windows looked onto the deep, still lake of a vast volcanic crater. Beyond the crater's rim lofty mountains reared their mist-shrouded peaks in awesome beauty. Amidst such natural loveliness the IPR Bureau had thrown up a huge, characterless building and surrounded it with a wasteland of storage sheds, landing field, hangars, and acres of unkempt grounds. Forzon regarded the neglected landscape with disgust and thought sympathetically of the legendary bird-in-space that bruised its wings against a vacuum.

The IPR base was a cultural vacuum.

Forzon contemplated its sterile hideousness and felt bruised.

Depressed by the drabness within, revolted by the view from his windows, Forzon spent some minutes in irate floor pacing and then flung himself from the room for a perfunctory tour of the building.

It had already occurred to him that for such an enormous establishment there were very few people about. The H-shaped building consisted of two two-storey dormitory wings connected by a long, single-storey section that housed the administrative and service rooms. Forzon passed by the reception room without a glance and prowled the full length of the lower corridor of the dormitory opposite his.

As he turned back he felt music.

13

Felt, rather than heard. The sound was so soft, so delicate, so indescribably fragile, that no single sense seemed to play a part in apprehending it. He stood transfixed and breathless before a door, and long after the sound had faded he imagined that he still heard it.

He waited, and when the music did not start again he knocked timidly.

The door opened and a girl stood before him – a startlingly feminine girl, her long hair a gleaming gold, her brightly colored robe a brilliant contrast to the severely furnished room behind her.

'I'm sorry,' Forzon said. 'I didn't know these were the women's quarters. I heard the music, and I was curious.'

To his amazement she glanced furtively up and down the corridor, drew him quickly into the room, and closed the door. Then, magically, her frowning expression softened to a smile. He took the chair she offered, and not until the smile broadened did he realize that he was staring at her.

'Sorry,' he said. 'All the women I've seen since I arrived here have been playing soldier.'

Her laughter, in some ethereal way, reminded him of the music he'd heard, but when she spoke she dropped her voice to a whisper. 'They're base personnel. They have to play soldier. I'm Team B.'

'Team B?' he echoed, matching her whisper.

'Resting up,' she went on. 'I caught a virus.'

Suddenly he noticed the instrument standing on a low table near her cot. It was similar to the one he'd seen in the portrait, but only two feet high and looking more like a child's toy than the medium for great art. Its wood frame was unadorned but richly polished.

'It's so small!' Forzon exclaimed. 'The one in the portrait was enormous!'

Her finger at her lips reminded him that he had raised his voice. 'That's a *torril*,' she said softly. 'A man's instrument. An instrument for public performance. The frame is elaborately carved and built precisely to the musician's

14

height. When the young *torril* player is growing up he must have a new instrument yearly. This one is a *torru*, a woman's instrument. Its tone is well-suited to the boudoir but is much too delicate for concert use.'

'A marvelous, whispering tone,' Forzon said. He got to his feet and bent over the *torru*. The slender strings were of some tightly twisted fiber, white and – every fifth string – black. He plucked them gently, one at a time. 'It's an inflected pentatonic scale!' he exclaimed. 'Primitive, and at the same time highly sophisticated. Curious.'

The girl was smiling at him again. 'I've wondered what CS men were like. Now I know. They hear music!'

She could have been poking fun at him, but Forzon answered her seriously. '*Culture* is such a broad concept that the Cultural Survey has to have more areas of specialization than you'd care to hear about. My own specialty is arts and crafts, and I'm a connoisseur of the utterly unique in any of them. This instrument, now. The circular arrangement of strings. Do you know that it defies classification?'

'I never thought of classifying it. It's a lovely instrument to play.'

'Play something,' Forzon suggested.

He watched her deft fingers and listened, absorbed and fascinated, until the last of the rippling, whispering tones had faded. 'Amazing,' he breathed. 'The technical facility is incredible. You have all of the strings right under your fingers, whereas with most species of harp—'

He paused. Footsteps had sounded in the corridor outside her door, and she stirred uneasily. 'It must be nearly lunchtime,' he said. 'Will you join me?'

She shook her head gravely. 'I think it would be best if no one knows we've been talking. So – please don't mention it to anyone.' She hurried him to the door, opened it cautiously, looked out. 'Don't come back here,' she whispered. 'I'll try to see you before I leave.'

Abruptly he was in the corridor again, walking away, and her door closed noiselessly behind him. He had turned the corner before he realized that she had not told him her name.

The wafting aroma of food drew him to the dining room, where he found his route to the food dispenser blocked by one of Coordinator Rastadt's female militia. 'Officers are served in their quarters,' she announced.

'That's very kind of you,' Forzon said absently. 'But I prefer to eat here.'

She flushed confusedly but held her ground with dogged determination. 'The coordinator has directed—'

'Tell him,' Forzon murmured, 'that the supervisor was hungry.'

He stepped around her, served himself, and carried his food to a long table where a number of young women in uniform and young men in work dress were already eating. He was received in silence; the other diners avoided his eyes and responded in mumbled monosyllables when he attempted to start a conversation. One by one they departed, and long before Forzon finished eating he was alone.

He returned to his quarters, where he found a lavish luncheon laid out on his work table. Disgustedly he emptied the congealed food into the disposal. He was dourly contemplating the blighted view from his windows when a knock sounded.

He measured his caller with one swift glance. This, he thought, has *got* to be the assistant coordinator.

The man snapped to attention and saluted. 'Assistant-Coordinator Wheeler reporting.'

Forzon told him to skip it and come in and sit down. And when he answered, 'Yes, sir,' Forzon told him to skip that, too. 'The name is Jef. Do you have a first name?'

'Blagdon.' Wheeler grinned foolishly. 'My friends call me Blag.'

'Good enough. I'd wear myself out saying Assistant-Coordinator Wheeler.'

Wheeler grinned again, handed Forzon a thick book,

and arranged himself comfortably on a chair. Forzon grinned back at him. Having met Coordinator Rastadt, he could have predicted his assistant. A big, easygoing, pleasant-looking man, his principal function on this base would be the soothing of feelings rumpled by his brusque superior.

Then Wheeler's grin faded, and Forzon realized with a start that the man had two faces, tragic and comic, and probably did not know himself whether he was a weeping clown or a laughing tragedian.

Forzon hefted the book. 'What's this?'

'Field Manual 1048K. The basic IPR manual. It tells you everything, which is probably a lot more than you'll want to know.'

Forzon pushed it aside. 'You're supposed to brief me.'

'Yes,' Wheeler agreed. 'But first – we've found your orders.'

'You've *found* them?'

Wheeler nodded unhappily. Even at his glummest his round, congenial face seemed about to break into laughter. Forzon regarded him sympathetically. Whatever abilities the man had, he was doomed to pass through life as someone's assistant. At every crisis in his career the clown in his character would rear its leering head and convince his superiors that this was not a man to be taken seriously.

'One of the communications men goofed,' Wheeler said. 'Not his fault, really. The orders were for someone he'd never heard of. He knew there was no Jef Forzon on Gurnil and no supervisor of any kind within light-years of here. Naturally he figured that the orders had been mistakenly coded for Gurnil, and he filed them and asked for confirmation. A lot of things can happen to an interspatial relay, and the confirmation never arrived – and your orders stayed filed. Anyway, there's no harm done. You're here, and your orders are here. I'm having copies made now. You're to take command of Team B.'

Forzon stared at him. 'A Cultural Survey officer in charge of an Interplanetary Relations Bureau field team?

17

You'd better refile those orders and send another request for confirmation.'

'I already have,' Wheeler said. 'I've asked for confirmation, I mean, but that's routine. I don't think there's any chance of an error.'

'Then someone in IPR Bureau Supreme Headquarters is crazy.'

For once Wheeler's smile was merely wistful. 'I've been contending that for years, but regardless of the mental condition of the person issuing them, orders are inevitably orders. Team B is yours.'

'To do what?'

'Mmm – yes. Some Gurnil history might be helpful to you.'

'Anything would be helpful.'

'To be sure. I was forgetting that you don't – that you're not—' He grinned mournfully and paused for a moment's thought. 'As you no doubt know, the Interplanetary Relations Bureau functions chiefly outside the boundaries of the Federation of Independent Worlds. As the Federation grows, IPR moves ahead and prepares the way for it. It charts space and explores and surveys the planets. If it discovers intelligent life a coordinator is appointed, and he establishes an IPR base, conducts a classification study, and sets up the field teams he needs to guide the planet toward membership in the Federation. If there is no intelligent life then various other things happen, none of which need concern us because Gurnil had two flourishing human-type civilizations when it was first surveyed four hundred years ago. Do you know anything about IPR procedures?'

Forzon shook his head. 'How could I? You don't let CS in until you certify a planet non-hostile, and you don't do that until your work is finished and the planet has actually applied for Federation membership.'

'We can't take a chance on having our work messed up,' Wheeler observed.

'Thanks,' Forzon said dryly. 'In the meantime, you mess up our work.'

Wheeler flashed his tragic grin. 'We have one or two things to think about other than culture. This guiding a planet toward Federation membership can be a touchy thing. There must be a planet-wide democratic government, set up by the people themselves without apparent outside interference. We have to work in a terrible complex of regulations.'

'Democracy imposed from without—' Forzon murmured.

'The Bureau's first law. We rarely find even a planet-wide government, let alone a democracy. So we guide smaller political units toward democratic government, and then we guide them toward combining into larger units, and eventually we have our planet-wide democracy. And of course it all has to be done without the people knowing we're around. Sometimes it takes centuries.'

'Which is why the cultures are tainted by the time you let us in.'

'We can't help that.'

'So what am I doing on Gurnil now?'

'I don't know,' Wheeler said frankly. 'I'm just trying to tell you what IPR is doing here. Gurnil is bicontinental, and at first contact both continents were political entities controlled by absolute monarchies. The Bureau's classification team estimated our job here at fifty years.'

'That was four hundred years ago?'

Wheeler nodded. 'Team A, here in Larnor, was immediately successful. Within a dozen years the monarchy had been replaced by a flourishing democracy. It's still flourishing. It's practically a model of its kind. Team B, over in Kurr, had no success at all. After four hundred years Kurr is no closer to democratization than it was when the planet was discovered. The contrary – the situation keeps getting worse. Each succeeding monarch consolidates his power a bit further. And that's where matters stand now.'

'So I'm to take command of Team B, and my mission is to convert Kurr to a democracy.'

'Without apparent outside interference,' Wheeler added with a grin. 'You'll want to take a look at the Team B file. You should know something about what's been tried before you start making plans of your own.'

'You said the problem has been going on for four hundred years.'

'Yes—'

'A lot of things can be tried in four hundred years.'

'The Team B file fills a room,' Wheeler said cheerfully.

'Further, since IPR must find the problem of Kurr irritating if not downright embarrassing, over the years it will have assigned some of its best men there, and they'll have applied every trick and device and maneuver they could think of. All of them failed, so now IPR is giving the job to a Cultural Survey officer. If we rule out insanity it still seems like a rather desperate measure.'

'Supreme Headquarters is desperate,' Wheeler agreed. 'The Federation boundary can't be drawn in loops and curlicues. Neither can there be a forbidden hunk of space inside the boundary. A world like Gurnil can hold up the admission of a whole sector of worlds and bring Federation expansion to a dead stop.'

'If Kurr is so tough, how does it happen that Larnor was a pushover?'

'Larnor is a poor continent, and it had an immensely stupid king. Its resources had been neglected. The people lived in dire poverty, and it didn't take much to incite them to revolt. The king was encouraged to impose more and more taxes, and the people were encouraged to do something about them.'

'All without outside interference, of course.'

'Without *apparent* outside interference. It's not quite the same thing.'

'What about Kurr?'

'An immensely wealthy continent, and its rulers have

20

been nothing short of brilliant. They're tyrants, with the usual evil vices of tyrants, but they've known to a hair just how far they can go without ruffling their subjects. Some refined instinct seems to keep a check on their natural greed, and they can acquire as much wealth as they think they need without oppressive taxation because their realm is so wealthy. They're even shrewd enough to temper their acts of cruelty. The king may summarily seize a girl who takes his fancy, but he always rewards her father or husband, and when he tires of her he rewards the girl. What should be an intolerable act of oppression becomes a highly profitable honor. If a subject offends him the king may have his left arm severed at the elbow – a favorite practice of the present King Rovva – but the victim will be pensioned off, and it's usually a court hanger-on about whom the people aren't likely to be concerned anyway. And naturally the people have had respect for the monarch bred into them for generations.'

'What about relations between Kurr and Larnor?'

'There haven't been any formal relations since the Larnorian revolt. The kings of Kurr were shrewd enough to see that Larnorian ideas were dangerous. Informally, the Larnorians used to send out missionaries to spread both their religion and democracy, but they always disappeared without a trace. Probably they ended up in the king's one-hand villages. Both continents are at technological level twenty, and ocean travel is brutally primitive. It wasn't difficult for Kurr to cut off virtually all contact.'

'You said that IPR works in a terrible complex of regulations. What are they?'

Wheeler gestured at IPR Field Manual 1048K.

Forzon pulled it toward him and flipped the pages. Emblazoned on the frontispiece and at the head of every chapter was the Bureau's first law: DEMOCRACY IMPOSED FROM WITHOUT IS THE SEVEREST FORM OF TYRANNY. Capsules of what the Bureau obviously considered distilled wisdom leaped out in bold, black capitals as Forzon turned the pages.

THE BUREAU DOES NOT CREATE REVOLUTION. IT CREATES THE NECESSITY FOR REVOLUTION. GIVEN THAT NECESSITY, THE NATIVE POPULATIONS ARE PERFECTLY CAPABLE OF HANDLING THE REVOLUTION.

DEMOCRACY IS NOT A FORM OF GOVERNMENT; IT IS A STATE OF MIND. PEOPLE CANNOT BE ARBITRARILY PLACED IN A STATE OF MIND.

THE RULE OF ONE WAS A MASTERFUL CONCESSION BECAUSE IT CONCEDED NOTHING. INCOMPETENT FIELD WORKERS AGITATED FOR THE SUBSTITUTION OF TECHNOLOGY FOR INTELLIGENCE. THEY WERE GIVEN TECHNOLOGY – IN A WAY THAT LEFT THEM ABSOLUTELY DEPENDENT UPON INTELLIGENCE.

ONE MEASURE OF THE URGENCY OF REVOLUTION IS THE FREEDOM THE PEOPLE HAVE, COMPARED WITH THE FREEDOM THEY WANT.

Forzon snapped the book shut. 'Catch,' he said, and lofted it to Wheeler, who clutched it awkwardly, his face contorted with bewilderment. He was the tragedian whose most telling pathos had inexplicably drawn a laugh. 'What – what are you going to do?'

'How long does it take a Bureau man to work his way through that morass of fine print?'

'Three years.'

'Surely it wasn't the intention of your superiors that I spend three years mastering Field Manual 1048K.' He got to his feet and strode to a window. Each time he saw it the blighted base area irritated him more. He wondered if the IPR personnel never looked beyond the conditioned confines of their building, never noticed this corrosion of the crater's grandeur. A Cultural Survey base would have been surrounded by as much beauty as devoted hands and obedient machines could coax from the environment.

He turned. 'Those paintings in the reception room. Are they from Kurr?'

22

Wheeler hesitated. 'I'm sure most of them are. I never thought to inquire.'

Forzon said caustically, 'If some of them are, then all of them are. Widely separated continents with few contacts don't develop identical artistic styles and techniques.'

He hadn't needed to ask. The girl with the *torru* was from Team B, meaning that she was from Kurr, and the *torru* was a miniature version of the elaborate instrument in the painting. 'And the natives don't know you're here,' Forzon mused. 'No wonder the coordinator flipped when I told him to bring in some musicians and artists. But how can you guide the people toward democracy if you have no contact with them?'

'But we do!' Wheeler protested indignantly. 'Every agent of a field team has a native role. You'll have to have one, too, before you can assume your command.'

'I see. Some kind of disguise, in other words.'

'Not a disguise. An *identity*.'

'If that's what you want to call it. I'm beginning to see a glimmer of light. The Bureau has a long-standing problem in Kurr. Kurr obviously has a fantastic level of cultural achievement. After four hundred years someone in the Bureau has finally noticed this and got to wondering if perhaps a Cultural Survey officer might be of some assistance. Very well. I've been placed in command of Team B. I'll go to Kurr, and I'll use Team B to set up a cultural survey.'

'Cultural –' Wheeler took a deep breath and finished on a falsetto '– survey?'

'That's what I'm trained to do. It'd be silly for me to begin with the IPR Field Manual. The only potential I'd have there is that in three years I might become as competent as a newly graduated IPR cadet – if I study diligently. In the absence of specific orders to the contrary, I can only assume that IPR wishes to fill in those gaps in its knowledge that occur in my area of specialization, and that

23

I was requisitioned to perform this task. Have you a better explanation for my assignment?'

Wheeler did not answer.

'I'll need a blitz language course,' Forzon said.

'Certainly. I'll send up the equipment. I'll also check into the matter of an identity for you.'

'I'd like to meet some of the members of Team B,' Forzon said, thinking of the girl with the *torru.*

Wheeler frowned. 'If you like. It'd be a little awkward, though. They're all established in Kurr, and they can't always break away at a moment's notice. They have to maintain their positions, or a lot of good work is wasted. We could bring back one or two at a time, but it would take forever for you to meet very many of them. It'd be much better if you saw them in Kurr.'

'Aren't there any Team B personnel here at base?'

'No,' Wheeler said easily. 'Team B once maintained a headquarters here, but all we have now is its archives, which are serviced by base personnel. All of Team B is in Kurr. We can fly you there whenever you're ready.'

He nodded pleasantly and left. Forzon's first impulse was to hurry over to the women's quarters, but a sober second thought checked him. The girl may have been concerned with proprieties when she told him not to come back to her room. Or she may have been giving him a warning.

THREE

On one point Forzon had gained some useful information. The Interplanetary Relations Bureau had always been run more like a secret order than a governmental department. Few people outside the Bureau knew what its function was, but anyone who worked and traveled along the space frontier quickly became aware that the Bureau's power there was absolute. It was said that even an admiral of the space navy asked IPR permission when he wanted to maneuver across a Federation boundary.

Now Forzon understood why. The Bureau's mission was to guide worlds to Federation membership, and to do so without those worlds being aware of it. Obviously this would be impossible if traders, explorers, scientists, various governmental surveys, and ships in distress – not to mention lost tourists – provided a rain of visitors from outer space. So the IPR Bureau policed the boundaries.

On Gurnil there was a continent, Kurr, still ruled by a monarch. The admission of neighboring, fully qualified worlds to the Federation had long been delayed; the Bureau was embarrassed. Understandably the situation called for drastic action, but someone at the Bureau's Supreme Headquarters had tripped over a panic button.

A Cultural Survey sector supervisor in charge of the Kurr field team? It was comparable to placing an IPR officer in charge of a Cultural Survey project, and from what Forzon had seen of the way the Bureau handled art he knew what that would lead to.

Since he had no idea what was expected of him, he determined to give the Bureau the one thing he understood: a cultural survey. He prepared specimen survey forms and handed them to Rastadt's secretary, requesting initial runs of a thousand. A day later the copy still lay untouched on the corner of her desk. Forzon spoke sharply to Wheeler, who shed cheerful tears and promised to duplicate them himself.

Forzon applied himself to the language course, studying constantly because he had nothing else to do, but his thoughts kept turning to the girl with the *torru*, the member of Team B who, according to Wheeler, did not exist. He wondered if he would ever see her again.

She came at night.

Forzon, awakened from a restless sleep by a cool hand

and her urgent whisper, sat up quickly and groped for a light.

'No light!' she whispered.

He heard the soft rustling of her gown, her quick breathing, caught the faint scent of an unknown perfume, but he could not see her.

'I fly back tomorrow,' she said.

'In the daytime? I thought the natives weren't supposed to know that IPR is here.'

'It'll be night in Kurr.'

'Of course. Did you know that I'm the new Team B commander? Perhaps I should go with you.'

'No!' she said quickly. Then she echoed, with an obvious note of incredulity, 'The new – *Team B commander?*'

'That's what my orders say.'

'That's very interesting.'

He attempted to conjure her image out of the room's thick darkness. He remembered her face perfectly – the smooth curve of her cheek and the delicate perfection of her turned-up nose as she bent in profile over the *torru*, frowning slightly in concentration on her nimble fingers.

'You shouldn't go back with me,' she said. 'It will be best if they don't know that we've met.'

'Have me met? I don't even know who you are.'

'Ann Cory. Officially, Gurnil B627.'

'All right, Gurnil B627. What do you do in Team B?'

'Among other things, I'm a music teacher in Kurra, which is the capital city of Kurr. I give music lessons to the talented and not-so-talented daughters of the elite.'

'How large is Team B?'

'About two hundred.'

'Two – *hundred?* I had no idea there were so many agents in Kurr. All of them masquerading as natives, I suppose.'

'Members of a Bureau team don't masquerade,' she said coldly. 'We *are* natives – when we're in Kurr.'

'I see. Two hundred. Spread over the whole country that probably isn't very many.'

'Didn't the coordinator brief you?'

'Wheeler gave me a manual, which I immediately gave back to him. He told me a little about the situation. I gather that the people of Kurr are perfectly satisfied with things as they are, or IPR wouldn't have labored in vain for four hundred years. Also that their King Rovva stubbornly refuses to take any action that would make them dissatisfied. My own ideas have a Cultural Survey bias and will probably sound treasonable to you, but it seems to me that if a people are satisfied and happy – and these Kurrians are, I can tell from the art they create – the IPR Bureau has no business contriving the overthrow of their government.'

'One of the things you must see in Kurr,' she said softly, 'are the one-hand villages. There are several of them, populated exclusively by men and women who have displeased the king and had their left arm severed at the elbow. It's a pleasant little diversion the king indulges in to amuse himself and his court. The attendant who sneezes when the king has ordained silence, or who drops a serving tray – but no one is immune, not even the king's high ministers. There are good kings and bad kings, and we in the Bureau sometimes find ourselves working to depose a king who is a kind, benevolent monarch and whom we personally like and admire. It's the system that's evil. The ideal monarch may have a monster for a successor.'

'Very well. The system is evil and must be changed, but by the people themselves. Democracy imposed from without—'

He paused. Her gown rustled softly as she shifted her feet, but she remained tantalizingly invisible. 'I'm working on the language,' he said. 'I'll have it down pretty well in another day, and I'll be fluent in two. It's an easy language – much easier than learning to walk in the dratted priest's

27

costume that your people picked out for me. I keep stumbling over it. I don't care much for that ghastly artificial nose, either, but if Kurrians are cursed with monumental snouts I suppose I'd be rather conspicuous without one.'

He did not presume to say it, but the one aspect of his assignment that he most dreaded was seeing Ann Cory wearing a disfiguring Kurrian nose.

'What priest's costume?' she asked.

Forzon sighed. 'I'm to be a sort of wandering holy man. Rastadt says they're quite common in Kurr, and it's an absolutely safe role because no native would dare to look twice at me, much less speak. But I suppose you know all about them.'

'Not really. They're not often seen in Kurra.'

'That's right. They avoid cities, which they consider cesspools of the unfaithful. Before I can go to Kurra I'll need an alternate identity. Do you have an alternate identity?'

'Of course. Every Team B agent has several identities.'

'That's encouraging. Eventually I'll be rid of that dratted robe, though I suppose I'll be stuck with the nose as long as I'm in Kurr.'

'I'd like to sample your linguistic ability,' she said.

He gave her a colloquial greeting, 'Hail, citizen,' and rambled on at length about the weather, the coming harvest, and how soon the province tax collector might be expected. She made no comment when he finished.

'What's the matter,' he asked. 'Is my accent bad?'

'No. Your accent is very good. Remarkable, considering the short time you've had to practice. My suggestion is that you wait three days, and then ask to be taken to Kurr.'

'Why three days?'

'Just a precaution. It'll give us time to get ready for you.'

'Team B knows that I'm coming. I'm to be put down at a remote station where there are no Holy Places that might require me to perform a religious function and very few natives for me to bless even if I feel benevolently inclined, which I won't. I can't start work until my forms are ready,

28

but no doubt I'll be able to pick up background information more quickly on the scene than I can here at base.'

'What forms?' she asked.

'The forms for my cultural survey.'

Again there was silence, broken only by the soft rustle of her gown. 'Wait three days,' she said finally. 'Don't tell anyone that you've talked with me. I'll see you in Kurr.'

She was gone. He did not even hear the door close after her.

'It has been wisely written,' Forzon murmured, 'that if one pursues an enigma far enough, inevitably one must come either to the beginning or to the end. Unfortunately the sage doesn't specify whether he means the end of the enigma or the end of the pursuer. I don't like this. It's bad enough to have the feeling that one is being used. It's insufferable not to know by whom, or to what purpose.'

He remained in his quarters the next day, concentrating furiously on the language. At intervals a uniformed young lady would thrust a heavily laden tray at him and depart with an unseemly haste that could only have been born of a fear that he might devour her instead of the food.

The following morning he strolled down to the administration section. The receptionist eyed him suspiciously; Forzon ignored her. He was becoming accustomed to suspicious glances. He went directly to the coordinator's office, where the secretary icily informed him that the coordinator was indisposed.

'Assistant-Coordinator Wheeler?' Forzon suggested.

'He's in the field today.'

'Team A or Team B?'

She shrugged; he wasn't interested enough to pursue the subject. He went to the room marked *Team B Head-quarters*, opened the door, looked in. The drab bindings of official records stood in solid ranks that filled the walls from floor to ceiling. Circular filing cabinets crammed the floor space; boxes were piled high on top of them. The place was a sepulcher for the desiccated remains of four centuries of failure.

Resolutely Forzon stepped back and closed the door. Just as he had no intention of investing years in the study of the IPR field manual, neither would he waste time in exhuming the futilities of Team B's past.

In the reception room he thoughtfully contemplated the paintings. They, too, were old, and had it not been for the filtered air and controlled humidity of the building he might be commencing his work on Gurnil with a tedious restoration of the IPR art collection.

'How long have these paintings been here?' he asked the receptionist.

She gazed at him blankly. 'I don't know, I'm sure.'

'What's the point of maintaining this base if its personnel know so little about Gurnil and care less?' Forzon demanded.

'The base serves as a supply depot and record depository,' the receptionist said primly.

'That's interesting,' Forzon remarked, keeping his eyes on the paintings. 'Then there must be very little to do, especially for a receptionist. I gather that the field agents rarely come here. The natives presumably don't know that the base exists, so they don't visit you. You'd have plenty of advance notice on supply contacts and visits from higher headquarters. I can't think of any reason why this base should need a receptionist.' He turned and gave her his most engaging smile. 'Could it be possible that you were appointed just to keep an eye on me?'

Her reaction, whatever it might be, was certain to be unattractive; so Forzon said over his shoulder, 'Please let me know when the coordinator is available,' and returned to his quarters.

Later Rastadt sent for him, greeted him with a scowl, and as an afterthought leaped to his feet to snap off a salute. 'They said you wanted to see me.'

'Can you arrange transportation to Kurr for me the day after tomorrow?' Forzon asked.

'Kurr? Why?'

'To take command of Team B. I'd rather not waste any more time here at base than is absolutely necessary.'

'You can command Team B from here,' Rastadt said. 'There's no reason for you to go to Kurr. None at all. And it'd be dangerous.'

'Strange that you should think so,' Forzon remarked. 'Only three days ago you were rehearsing me in the role of a Kurrian priest.'

'That was just a demonstration. I'm not turning you loose in Kurr until you've been trained in everything a Kurrian priest needs to know. At the first opportunity we'll bring back a Team B agent who's had actual experience in the role. Until he convinces me that you're competent, you'll have to command Team B from here.'

'You wouldn't be turning me loose there,' Forzon protested. 'I'll be exposed only between the landing area and the Team B station and it'll be dark anyway. Wheeler said the costume was only a precaution.'

'It isn't precaution enough. The IPR field teams owe their success to the fact that nothing is left to chance. I can't permit you to incur such a risk.'

Forzon said coldly, 'I believe, Coordinator, that this is my decision to make.'

'Not at all. You outrank me by four grades, but the co-ordinator of a planet has full responsibility for the safety of all IPR personnel, of whatever rank or status.'

'Has Wheeler returned yet?'

'I believe so. Why?'

'Call him in here.'

Rastadt irritably snapped an order at his communicator. Wheeler strolled in a moment later, nodded cheerfully at Forzon, and asked, 'What's the problem?'

Rastadt glared at him. 'Don't *you* know how to report to a sector supervisor?'

Wheeler flushed, muttered an apology, saluted. Forzon felt too embarrassed to intervene.

'No wonder this planet is a mess,' Rastadt growled. 'No one does anything right.'

Forzon said to Wheeler, 'Did you, or did you not, tell me I could go to Kurr whenever I was ready?'

'I – yes—'

'I'm ready.'

The coordinator leaned forward. 'Assistant-Coordinator Wheeler, would you kindly cite for me the regulation under which *you* have been delegating *my* authority?'

'But I did ask you about it, sir, and you said—'

'I said the supervisor could go to Kurr whenever he was ready. I did *not* say he could go whenever he *thought* he was ready. A novice from another governmental department, whatever his rank, has no competence to make such decisions. An IPR man is not ready to take the field until he has been thoroughly trained and indoctrinated, and if you aren't aware of that by now the planet Gurnil is badly in need of a new assistant coordinator. What are you trying to do – blow the planet?'

Wheeler, his large face now white and oozing perspiration, opened and closed his mouth soundlessly. In another moment he would have been cringing, and a cringing clown was something that Forzon did not care to see. He said, 'Coordinator, I think it's time that we asked Supreme Headquarters to clarify the command situation here. Will you make the request, or shall I?'

Rastadt leaped to his feet, stood for a long moment poised to unleash his rage at Forzon – and then crumpled. 'I'll – make the request,' he muttered.

'Thank you,' Forzon said.

He returned their salutes and left them.

Wheeler, panting heavily, overtook him in the corridor outside his quarters. 'It's all right,' the assistant coordinator gasped. 'I'll have transportation ready for you whenever you want it.'

'Day after tomorrow?'

'If you like.'

'Why the sudden change?'

Mopping his brow, Wheeler said nervously, 'Let's go where we can talk.'

Forzon led him into his quarters, got him seated, and remarked, 'You need a drink. Sorry I can't offer you one.'

Wheeler mopped his brow again. 'Not permitted on this base. Coordinator's orders.' He looked woundedly at Forzon, and both of them burst into laughter.

'I want to ask you a favor,' Wheeler said suddenly. 'A Bureau field team is autonomous, but its commander works under the general supervision of the planet's coordinator. This raises an awkward question. You are the ranking officer on this planet. At the same time the tables of organization make you subordinate to the coordinator because you command a field team. It's a peculiar situation, and as you've noticed, your orders don't clarify it.'

'What do you suggest?'

'That you don't make an issue of it. Observe the traditional command setup and submit your plans to the coordinator for approval as any team commander would do. The coordinator will approve them as a matter of course, I'm sure. There's no harm in letting him pretend, is there? He's really a fine old man with a distinguished career behind him, but he had the misfortune of drawing an impossible assignment.'

'He impresses me as being thoroughly irascible.'

'Naturally he feels frustrated. Kurr has broken a lot of coordinators, and he doesn't want to end his service with a failure on his record.'

Forzon said politely, 'Since I know nothing about IPR regulations, I see nothing unreasonable about having my plans reviewed carefully by someone who does.'

'Splendid!' Magically, Wheeler was the clown again.

'But I do insist on getting away from this base,' Forzon went on. 'I couldn't work effectively here. Besides, there's

33

a conspiracy to keep me out of the dining room, and your base personnel refuse to speak to me.'

Wheeler fluttered a hand indifferently. 'They're probably afraid of you. You're the highest ranking officer most of them have ever seen. Day after tomorrow, then. You can't take anything with you, you know.'

'Nothing at all?'

'Nothing,' Wheeler said firmly. 'You can't have anything on your person that a Kurrian priest wouldn't have, and that's very little. We use special planes for our contacts with Kurr. They aren't very fast, but they're virtually noiseless. We have to put our agents down on lightly populated stretches of coast where we aren't likely to inspire any local superstitions. Put them down and run – there are night fishermen who work closely inshore, and it wouldn't do to have one happen onto the plane. The coordinator is notifying Team B now, so there'll be someone on hand to meet you. There is one thing. He doesn't think you should go, but since you insist on it he insists on going with you.'

'There's nothing wrong with that, is there?'

'I suppose not.'

'Why shouldn't the coordinator go to Kurr?' Forzon persisted.

'No special reason. I'd feel better if you had an experienced agent with you. I'd hoped to go myself. I'm a former member of Team B, and I know Kurr. Not that it really matters. You'll be put down close to a Team B station, and you'll be met. Anyway, Coordinator Rastadt insists that it's his responsibility.'

'Isn't it?' Forzon asked politely.

'I suppose it is. But you see – he's never been to Kurr.'

FOUR

They approached the coast at low altitude and circled once. The onshore wind of evening had faded; a scattering of slowly drifting clouds fitfully obscured Gurnil's tiny moon, and at first the land below looked appallingly dark and hostile. They circled a second time, and as they moved out over the sea again Forzon, looking back, picked out an isolated light and – in a valley beyond – the dimly diffused glow from a fog-shrouded village.

Rastadt had been talking in low tones with the pilot. 'It looks all right,' he announced. 'Take her down.'

They descended vertically, bounced, and came to rest. Forzon jumped out and found himself on a narrow strip of sandy beach. Waves broke rhythmically, running up the beach to lap at his sandals.

Rastadt scrambled down beside him, robe flapping awkwardly, sending whistling snorts through the upward curve of his disfiguring artificial nose. 'There isn't much tide,' he said. 'Just enough to remove any suspicious marks.' He moved away from the plane and called out guardedly. 'Someone should be here to meet us,' he muttered.

He trotted off along the shore, wheeled, trotted back again. His white robe caught the dim moonlight and made a flouncing specter of him. 'We're early,' he said, 'but they should have been here. Damn! Wouldn't do to have a fisherman happen along.'

He spoke briefly with the pilot and turned away with a gesture of impatience. 'Come on,' he said to Forzon.

A low bluff overhung the beach. Rastadt, muttering that there was supposed to be a path somewhere, blundered about in the darkness and finally began a stumbling, uncertain climb. Forzon gathered his robe about him and followed. At the top Rastadt paused and waited, panting, until Forzon caught up with him. Ahead of them was the deeper gloom of a thick forest, but beyond, high on a distant hill, the solitary light still burned brightly.

'Farmhouse,' Rastadt announced. 'Team B station. They should have met us.'

Forzon studied the light calculatingly. Distances were deceptive at night; he guessed two miles, three at the most, and hoped it was no more than four. Behind him he could dimly make out the empty beach below. The plane had vanished silently.

'Aren't you going back?' he exclaimed.

'I was, but I can't leave a confounded novice wandering about in a strange country. They should have met us. Damn!' He was still panting, gasping his words. 'The plane'll come for me tomorrow night. We shouldn't have any trouble finding the place. It's the only house between here and the village, and there's the light. Let's go.'

Forzon took a step, caught a toe in his robe, and stumbled. 'Don't do that!' Rastadt snapped.

'Sorry,' Forzon said.

'All you have to do is go about with an other-worldly expression on your face, and no one will dare question your presence. But if you start getting tangled up as though you've never worn a robe before—'

'I'll manage all right,' Forzon said.

'Come on. We'll probably meet them along the way.'

He turned, stumbled over his own robe, and moved on in silence.

They picked their way blindly through the trees until finally they encountered the narrow open space and ruts of a road. The distant light was blocked off by thick foliage, and Forzon could see nothing at all.

'From here we can follow the road,' Rastadt observed.

'If you can see where it goes, go ahead and follow it,' Forzon said.

As they hesitated the undergrowth about them thrashed

and erupted, unseen hands clutched at Forzon, and a heavy object brushed his head and struck his shoulder a glancing blow. Twisting instinctively Forzon seized an assailant and sent him crashing into others. Cries rang out, and a scream of pain. A voice shouted something that could have been a command. Forzon eluded another pair of groping hands, took several quick sidesteps, and slipped back into the trees.

Confusion boiled behind him. A torch flamed up suddenly, and in its flickering light he made out uniformed men in knee-length cloaks. He edged away as rapidly as he dared, cursing thick undergrowth that rustled and snapped with every step.

His one thought was to go for help. He fancied himself capable of whatever bravery might be required of him, but the ambush of two men in the dark by an army was not a situation where bravery could have influenced the outcome. Forzon fled, making for the Team B station as directly as the tangled forest permitted. If Rastadt escaped he would certainly do the same; if he were captured Team B had to be told quickly. Its agents must be warned before they fell into the same trap.

The night sounds were dazzling. Trees sighed audibly at the faintest touch of wind, strangely musical insects sounded sporadic choruses, and a night bird sang a weirdly human cry of horror. Floundering forward with desperate haste, Forzon soon left the thrashing pursuit far behind.

The forest came to an abrupt end. Forzon turned aside and found the road again, and broke into a run. The moon came out, its faint light caressing his white robe with luminescence. Unwilling to pause even long enough to remove it, he gathered it closely about him and ran on. To his right was a cultivated field; to his left what seemed to be a pasture, with a crude wood fence that followed the road. He ran with short strides, stumbling frequently over the narrow ruts, ran until he could run no longer and still pressed forward, breathing with panting sobs. He was

37

climbing the last, long slope to the Team B station and could make out the dark shape of the house on the crest of the hill when suddenly the light went out.

At the top of the rise he staggered to a halt and stood looking about him uncertainly. In the valley beyond a few lights still showed ghost-like through the clinging fog. The farmhouse stood only a few paces from the road, dark and foreboding even in the fleeting moments when the moon showed, but its shape reassured Forzon. He recognized its quaint architecture from the paintings he'd seen at base: the curving outward flare of walls topped with a humped roof. He approached it resolutely, stumbled down two low steps that led to a sunken entrance, took a deep breath, and knocked.

Abruptly the insect noises ceased, and a bird choked off its cry and fluttered from the rooftop. Eerie silence closed in on him.

He knocked again.

The door opened. A man stood before him, lighted taper held aloft in one hand. He wore only a skirt-like garment, and the flickering light reflected palely from his bare chest and arms. For a suspenseful instant he peered incredulously at Forzon. Then he threw up his free hand as if to protect himself, uttered a sharp cry, and dropped the taper.

Forzon, his mind on the pursuit that must follow momentarily, leaped inside, picked up the sputtering taper, and closed and barred the door. He asked in Galactic and then in Kurrian, 'Who's in charge here?' The man backed away slowly, his face rigid with terror, his wide-open mouth gurgling inanities. A woman darted forward carrying a child. She sank to the floor with a shriek and raised one hand importuningly. The wide-eyed child added its own piping cry.

Helplessly Forzon glanced about the room, wasting precious seconds in a desperate effort to extract meaning from an utterly incomprehensible situation. The frantic convolutions of his thoughts tossed out one wild surmise after another, and each staggered him more than the preceding.

This was not a Team B station.

The man did not understand him; he remembered with a start that orders had been shouted at the ambush and he had not understood them.

These people possessed noses as normally proportioned as his own.

He was not in Kurr.

His now panicky gaze swept the room again and focused on the far wall, where the flickering light barely made discernible the outlines of several paintings. Holding the taper aloft, he moved closer. Magnificent paintings.

He was in Kurr.

The natives did not understand him, nor he them; the language he spoke was not Kurrian.

In one intuitive flash he perceived the damnable enormity of Rastadt's treachery. The coordinator had given Forzon the wrong language, clothed him in an alien costume that would terrify the natives, outfitted him with an atrocious artificial just in case the other stigmata did not suffice, led him into an ambush, and quietly disappeared. Had it not been for the flukish interaction of darkness and confusion Forzon would even now be on his way to involuntary retirement in one of King Rovva's one-hand villages.

With a seething pursuit just behind him, he could not remain where he was.

He had nowhere to go.

The man's eyes were riveted hypnotically to Forzon's face, to the looping disfigurement of the artificial nose. The woman was staring at his robe. He recognized her expression. He had seen it often, in art galleries, at concerts – a rapt admiration of beauty.

The robe was beautiful. Gleaming threads of gold interlaced its creamy white fluff. Its marvelous softness possessed a sheen that reflected a glowing halo in the feeblest light.

Forzon wrenched the outsized nose from his face, threw

it to the floor, ground it under the heel of his sandal, stomped on it. It held its shape. Dismayed, he snatched it up again and dropped it into the hot ashes of a metal brazier that stood on a table. It did not burn, but in an instant it melted into a shapeless mass. He seized a pair of tongs and raked the ashes over it.

Then he placed the taper in a wall bracket and calmly removed his robe.

The woman watched him open-mouthed; the man continued to gurgle hysterically. Forzon folded the billowing garment into a bundle, approached the woman, bowed low. 'Here,' he said grimly. 'You admire it? It's yours.'

She remained motionless, staring at him dumbly, so he placed the bundle on the floor in front of her and backed away. He was wearing only the short shift that had been given to him for an undergarment, and he felt chilled and not a little ridiculous.

The man was gazing at the robe as though he had just noticed it. He said something; the woman answered and placed the child on the floor so she could extend a hand timorously and stroke the lustrous cloth. The man drew closer, and they began to talk excitedly.

Voices lashed out suddenly beyond the door. Three sharp knocks sounded. The man and woman stared at each other, stared at Forzon. The knocks sounded again; a coarse voice bellowed a command.

The woman gathered up the robe. She hissed something at the man, who raised his arms as if to remonstrate. She darted away, cradling the robe like a sleeping babe. Then she turned, hissed at Forzon, gestured.

He stepped around the child and leaped after her.

In the next room she motioned him up a vertical ladder and awkwardly followed at his heels, clutching the robe with one hand. Behind them the man had opened the door upon a strident chorus of angry voices. Forzon emerged in darkness, took a few cautious steps, hesitated; the woman brushed past him, hissing urgently. He stumbled over a pallet, regained his balance, and moved after her.

A soft creaking sounded, and she pushed him forward roughly. He bumped his head and stooped through a low opening. The creaking sounded again.

He felt about him blindly. He was in a narrow space close under the arching roof. He could neither stand erect nor lie down, so he seated himself with legs crossed, leaned back against a wall, and waited. His cramped position on the hard floor quickly became painful, but in the comforting embrace of darkness his tension slowly drained away. The voices below were too faint to seem menacing, and finally the thump of the closing door brought silence. He succumbed to exhaustion and fell asleep.

He awoke with numbed limbs and bruised muscles, cold and hungry, but he scarcely noticed his discomfort. An overwhelming anger consumed him – anger at Rastadt, Wheeler, Ann Cory, Gurnil B627, the IPR Bureau, and the land of Kurr.

His hiding place was dimly lit by a wide, inverted V cut through the wall at a slight downward angle. In the paintings he had mistaken such marks for ornaments, but this one was obviously functional as well, designed to admit a bit of light and air but keep out the worst of the weather. He scrambled to his knees and peered out.

He saw only a very ordinary sweep of countryside, a strip of impoverished farmland crowded against the coast by steep, barren-looking hills.

'This is the fabulously wealthy land of Kurr?' he exclaimed.

He turned his attention to his more immediate surroundings. He was in a narrow cubicle, surrounded on three sides by straight walls and on the fourth by the sharply curving outer wall of the house. The roof arched just above his head. The walls seemed solid, and he found no clue as to how he had entered until he felt along the base of an interior wall and discovered that one wide plank was hung on a high pivot. Its own weight kept it in place, and pressure from the room beyond would not move it unless applied high up on the wall.

All of which was interesting but not especially helpful. He was still hungry, sore, cold – and angry.

Time passed. He submerged himself in a painstaking review of everything that had happened since he arrived on Gurnil, but no fact that he could recall cast any light on the incredible situation in which he found himself: the Team B station that was not, the Kurrians who had neither the right language nor the proper noses, the mystery of his priestly robe, the coordinator's conduct.

The plank creaked and dropped back into place with a soft thud. A deep, cylindrical bowl had been thrust into his hiding place. A single-pronged eating implement protruded from the top. Forzon sniffed hungrily, jabbed the implement into the bowl, speared something. It was a small ball of bread with a thick, chewy crust. His next thrusts brought up pieces of meat and vegetable, and as he ate he sipped the thick, steaming, gravy-like sauce. It had a strange, sweet-sour taste, but he consumed it with relish.

When he had finished he pushed up the swinging plank and crawled out. The upper storey was divided into two rooms by a wide partition that contained closets and – concealed next to the outer wall – his hiding place. Forzon circled both rooms, peering through the inverted V slits. The village, reposing peacefully in the valley below, looked deserted. So did the road that he had followed the night before, a faintly marked clutter of overgrown ruts. An outbuilding, a diminutive architectural echo of the house, stood a short distance to the rear. A strange-looking beast rested its huge, ugly head on a half door and gazed placidly at the nothing of the landscape. All seemed bleakly serene and uninteresting.

The woman heard him moving about and came clawing up the ladder in panic. There followed a frustrating pantomime in which Forzon plucked futilely at his flimsy shift

42

and tried to convey the information that he wanted clothing. At first the woman watched dumbly, and even after he was certain that she understood him she remained sullenly unresponsive. Finally, reluctantly, she went to the side of the room opposite his hiding place, raised a wall plank, and offered him – his robe.

He refused it with loud protestations and much arm waving, which brought her husband scrambling up the ladder. The man wore a knee-length, sleeveless shirt with a large, flapping collar that covered his arms like a cape. Beneath the shirt he wore an ankle-length skirt. Forzon plucked at this costume and performed more pantomime, and eventually they understood and brought clothing.

They left him, and he dressed himself and squatted on the floor to look through one of the slits at the village. For an hour or more he resolutely confronted the realities of his situation, and when he finished he had accomplished nothing: he could not remain where he was, he still had no place to go, and he could not think what to do about it.

He cautiously descended the ladder. The naked child was playing in a net suspended from the ceiling; she gazed at him with a wide-eyed, coy charm, and gurgled and cooed when he made faces at her. The woman was at work in the fields, driving the ungainly beast ahead of a farm implement. The man was nowhere to be seen.

The paintings caught Forzon's eyes, and he moved a bench to the corner of the room and sat down to study them admiringly. Art of that quality, in an ordinary farmhouse!

There were only seven. One, a portrait of a man and woman, was quite old and badly in need of restoration. Another, a landscape featuring the familiarly shaped mushroom house, was probably an old painting of this farm. The others were portraits and family groups; the most recent, of Forzon's host and his wife, was so new that the paint scarcely seemed dry. Its color was laid on with a flashy but decidedly inferior technique that made Forzon

43

apprehensive that the high craftsmanship of Kurrian art that produced the earlier paintings had declined or been stifled by oppressive monarchs.

But such paintings, in such a place! Forzon awesomely contemplated the implications of a culture where every peasant possessed his own art gallery.

Time passed; a distant creaking dissipated his reverie. The child was watching him quietly. The position of the sun marked the time as late afternoon. He had squandered several hours on seven paintings! Chagrined, he gave them a final, searching look to see if he could somehow justify his wholly unwarranted flight from reality, and exclaimed, 'The noses!'

The noses in these portraits were normally proportioned. So had been the noses in the portraits at base. He knew that the paintings came from Kurr, and yet he had allowed himself to be inveigled into wearing a grotesquely shaped snout to make him look Kurrian.

'The coordinator sized me up for the fool that I am,' he mused ruefully.

The creaking became louder. Forzon made a circuit of the unshuttered windows but could not locate the source. He climbed to the upper storey and saw a group of soldiers moving up the hill from the village, escorting a cart pulled by the same species of lumbering beast that the peasants owned. The loud creaking emanated from the cart's wood axles.

When they came closer Forzon saw that the cart had two passengers. One, a man, lay supine and motionless in the cart bed. The other, rigid on a plank seat at the front of the cart, was a stout, red-faced woman. Both were dressed in peasant costume. Neither seemed worth a second glance, but Forzon scrutinized them intently on the assumption that peasants accorded a military escort were no ordinary peasants.

These weren't. The man he had never seen before, but the woman, when she was close enough to be observed in

44

profile, displayed a pertly turned up nose and delicate curve of cheek that no casual disguise could conceal from an eye trained to aesthetic evaluations of lines and shapes.

It was Ann Cory, Gurnil B627, and Forzon's start of recognition jolted several pieces into place in the highly complex puzzle in which he was enmeshed. Obviously two members of Team B had attempted to meet him and had been lost to the same treachery that almost entrapped Forzon. Ann's feet were bound and her hands tied behind her. Her companion was also bound.

Moving from slit to slit, Forzon watched the cart until it disappeared into the distant forest. When finally it vanished he understood little more about the situation than he had that morning, but at least he knew what he had to do.

He prowled fretfully about the lower rooms, wasting precious minutes, until he found what he wanted – a knife. Doubtless there were other things that would have been useful to him, but he could think only of Ann's bound hands and feet. The half-moon disk of metal looked deceptively crude; its uneven edge was keen enough to draw blood when Forzon tested it with his thumb. He found to his disgust that he had no pockets, so he folded the knife into his cape.

He grimaced a farewell at the child – whom he sincerely hoped his brief visit would not render an orphan – sent a last, fleeting glance at the paintings, and fled the house.

He knew instinctively that any stranger traveling this road on this day would be suspect – why else had two experienced Team B agents been captured? – but he did not dare wait for darkness. The ill-marked road might have sudden turnings for him to miss and forks that would force desperate choices upon him, and with the safety of Ann Cory and her fellow agent at stake he could only strive to keep the cart in sight and damn the risk.

He ran.

When he reached the forest he paused to catch his breath and listen. Already the creaking cart had passed beyond

45

hearing, and the forest seemed oppressively still and threatening. There was no breeze; the trees' large, ovular leaves, so audible the night before, drooped in motionless silence.

Looking up at them, Forzon made a discovery. Every tree trunk grew straight to a height of ten feet or so and then made an identical curve. He had found both the inspiration for the outward curving walls of Kurrian architecture and the technical means for achieving them. He could recall no better example of the direct influence of a building material on architectural design. In fact—

The cart. Either he had taken longer than he realized, or the cart had stopped. He left the road and cautiously picked his way through the thick undergrowth.

The going was difficult, and he had to move with tortuous care to avoid ruffling the heavy silence. On and on he went, perspiring, laboriously parting the undergrowth ahead of him, stopping frequently to listen for the cart. Finally convinced that his tedious progress would never overtake it, he was about to risk the road again when he heard a distant shout. A few more steps brought him to the edge of the forest, and he dropped to the ground, parted a clump of shrubbery, and looked out.

Spread out on the slope beyond was a military encampment, with several carts drawn up, draught animals lolling complacently in the shade, a cooking fire, scattered heaps of straw that could have been beds. He counted eleven soldiers standing about the fire awaiting their turns at the food caldron.

There was no sign of Ann Cory and her companion.

The encampment looked as if it had been there for several days. He had seen no fires from the plane, but soldiers accustomed to chill nights and comfortably bedded down in straw would not maintain night fires. Grudgingly he had to concede that the ambush could have been accidental, a freakish coincidence in which they blundered into a squad of soldiers.

In that case where was the coordinator?

'He was outfitted just like me,' Forzon muttered. 'Nose, robe – language? Maybe Kurr has more than one language, and its people more than one type of nose, and we landed in the wrong place. But this isn't the time for solving riddles. Where's Ann? They didn't take her back the way they came, or I would have heard them. They didn't head for the hills, or they'd still be in sight. Most likely that's her escort waiting to be fed, and a relief squad took the cart north on the coastal road. In that case I'd better go north – and fast.'

He could not by-pass the camp on the land side without a time consuming and dangerous circuit. He turned toward the sea, descended the bluff he had climbed with Rastadt, and ran along the narrow beach until he had put the camp far behind him.

The bluff had increased in height. He contined to move forward, searching for a place where it could be climbed. Dusk was at hand when he finally made his way to the top and regained the road.

It had emerged from another thick growth of forest to run along a narrow shelf of stony waste where the hills advanced to meet the sea. He could see far up the coast to a point where the sea cliff gradually diminished and the road descended to veer off across a lovely farming country. The cart was not in sight.

Forzon told himself confidently that the ungainly beast's lurching gait could not have taken it beyond the horizon. He turned back, entered the already darkening forest, and pressed into thick, clinging undergrowth to wait.

Soon he heard the cart, its high-pitched creaking slowly crescendoing to an ear-splitting racket as it approached. Through a gap in the foliage he had a dim glimpse of the slobbering beast's head and the flapping cloaks of three plodding soldiers.

Only three. Momentarily Forzon felt heartened; but when the procession had passed from the forest into fading daylight and he was able to look again, he counted an escort

47

of seven. Ann still sat erect at the front of the cart. Her companion, if he was still with her, was hidden by the sideboards.

Forzon seated himself at the edge of the forest and watched the cart until it vanished into the swiftly gathering dusk. Then he started off in pursuit.

As full darkness closed in on him he saw a light flickering on the road far ahead. He broke into a stumbling run and almost overtook the cart before he realized that one of the soldiers was moving ahead of it with a torch. The others plodded beside the cart, three on either side, vaguely silhouetted by the shallow light.

The small moon was a spark on the sea's horizon, too low in the sky for its feeble glow to matter. Forzon stalked the cart, and while his mind groped for a plan of attack his foot stumbled over the weapon he needed. A stone. Immediately he perceived a ready-made strategy. The soldiers were hypnotized by the darkness, by the flickering torch, by the steady, deafening creaking of the cart, by the deadly monotony of this assignment that sent seven men to guard two bound prisoners. Unable even to speak to each other without shouting, they moved at a steady, mechanical pace, their eyes fixed rigidly ahead of them, their minds focused anywhere but on the dark road behind.

One soldier was so lost in thought that he lagged a pace behind the cart. Forzon moved up boldly, clouted him on the back of the head, and crouched over him to strike again if he moved. The others marched on. Even had they been alert they could have heard nothing above the cart's incessant caterwaul and seen nothing in the darkness that pressed in closely on the torch's light; and they were not alert.

Forzon stripped the thongs from his victim's sandals and bound his hands and feet securely. He rolled him off the road into a clump of grass. Overtaking the cart again, he measured another victim and left him bound and unconscious.

It seemed suspiciously easy. By the time he had dispatched four of the escort he was soaked with perspiration and sick with apprehension that his nervousness would cause him to blunder just short of success. The remaining soldiers were marching close to the light, and he doubted that he could attack one without the others noticing. He swung the stone; the soldier dropped. Forzon waited tensely until the cart had creaked past him, and then fumbled for the thongs.

With the odds against him reduced to two, Forzon became overconfident, struck a glancing blow, and had to strike again as his victim reeled and turned toward him. The soldier with the light was as hypnotized as the others; he never looked back.

At the crucial moment he might. Forzon hauled himself into the cart from the rear, edged past the man who lay there, and carefully applied his knife to the binding on Ann's hands. If he blundered with that last soldier he wanted her free to escape on her own.

She showed no surprise, made no movement except to lean back and place her lips to his ear. 'Who is it?'

He spoke the answer into her ear. 'Forzon.'

'*Forzon?*'

Her hands were free. He reached around her to sever the binding on her ankles, and then he turned to her companion. So shallow was the man's breathing that at first Forzon thought he was dead. He did not move when Forzon freed his hands and feet.

Ann placed her lips to his ear and spoke a single word. 'Hurry!'

Forzon eased himself to the ground and strode forward to strike what he hoped would be his final blow. The soldier dropped, the torch fell sputtering, the beast halted. The cart's creaking stopped so abruptly that Forzon's ears rang with the sudden silence.

'Don't let the torch go out,' Ann called.

He thrust it into the ground while he tied up the soldier, and then he went to join her. She was already signaling with a communicator that she took from a secret cavity in the cart bed. 'Six-two-seven. Emergency,' she said.

'Go ahead, six-two-seven.'

'I have the package. Emergency medical contact requested.'

'The package is—'

'Not the package.'

'I see. I'm alone here. How serious is it?'

'Critical,' she said flatly. 'Tomorrow night won't do.'

'Pick a landing place. I'm on my way.'

The cart's false bottom yielded a kit of medical supplies and a flask of water, and Ann cut away blood-soaked clothing and bathed and bandaged a gaping wound in the man's side.

'What happened?' Forzon asked.

'A soldier ran a spear through him. He needs a transfusion, but this is as much as we can do for him here.'

She stepped back from the cart and glanced about her, frowning, tapping one foot impatiently. She looked and acted the part of a tough, confident peasant woman, and Forzon, vividly remembering the fragile femininity she had displayed at base, found himself gaping at her bewilderedly.

'It isn't wise to bring the plane down in the open so close to habitations,' she said. 'We'll have to turn back.'

'Habitations?'

He had not noticed them, so intent had he been on stalking the cart. They had passed into the rich agricultural country, and the light of a farmhouse glimmered dimly a short distance ahead of them. 'I hope the soldiers I've tied up don't get loose and feel vengeful,' Forzon said.

'We'll have to turn them loose,' she announced.

'Turn them—'

'This is a lightly traveled road. If we don't they may never be found, and if they are found they'll immediately receive one-way tickets to the nearest one-hand village. King Rovva finds enough victims without Team B's assistance.'

'If you think it's safe.'

'They'll immediately head south,' she said confidently. 'There's a swampy jungle there where fugitives can hide until their alleged offenses have been forgotten. Team B keeps an agent there to help them. As far as we're concerned, the more fugitives the better.' She strode to the front of the cart and slapped the beast on its flank. 'This is an *esg*. It won't move at night unless someone goes ahead with a light.'

They turned the cart in a tight circle. Forzon released the last soldier, who was still unconscious, and then marched ahead with the torch, searching the roadside for his victims. All but two were unconscious, and those two, prompted by a few Kurrian words from Ann, headed south at the best gait their unsteady feet could manage.

When they reached the sea Ann picked out a likely stretch of beach, and they stripped the cart of its secret equipment. Leaving Ann with the wounded man, Forzon led the *esg* into the forest, forced it and the cart back into the trees as far as possible, and turned it loose. When daylight came it would wander about until some peasant claimed it.

He returned at a run to find the plane waiting and the wounded man already aboard. They took off at once and flew low over the sea with the coast a long, dark smudge where the water's phosphorescence ended.

Ann turned to him abruptly. 'How did you escape?'

'By not being captured,' he said.

She regarded him incredulously. 'The language they gave you was Larnorian. You were wearing the robe of a Larnorian priest, and Larnorian priests are the bogymen in all the Kurrian fairy tales. You had a Larnorian nose. Even if the district hadn't been full of soldiers you wouldn't have lasted an hour. Where'd you get the peasant clothing?'

'I traded my robe for it.'

'You *what?*'

'Traded—'

'You couldn't have! No Kurrian would touch it. If the king's ruffs caught a peasant with the robe of a Larnorian priest, they'd remove more than his arm. The peasants know that. Where'd you get the clothing?'

'I told you. Did you see any sign of the coordinator?'

'*Rastadt?*'

Forzon nodded. 'So much has happened that I nearly forgot him. We were together when the soldiers jumped us. I didn't see him after that. At first I thought he'd led me into a trap, but now I'm not so sure. He was dressed the same way I was.'

She said coldly, 'I didn't see any sign of him. Neither did anyone else.'

'That's odd.'

'I suppose he traded his robe for a uniform and joined King Rovva's army,' she said sarcastically. 'Where'd you get the clothing?'

He did not answer, and she did not speak again. Forzon dozed off and woke suddenly when the deep hum of the motor altered pitch. The land had thrust a long, narrow peninsula across their path. A light blinked below, and they circled, lost speed, and sank quickly downward. The ground opened to receive them.

They came to rest in an underground hangar. Eager hands reached in to lift out the wounded man, and then Ann jumped down. Forzon followed her and stood blinking in the hangar's bright lights.

'So this is the supervisor,' a young man said, pumping Forzon's hand.

'He says he's the supervisor,' Ann said coldly.

The young man arched his eyebrows. 'Says?'

'He's left several things unsaid, and several things he has said need a lot of explaining. I want him confined until Paul gets back – just in case.'

FIVE

Paul Leblanc was a man who had assumed so many identities that he no longer had one of his own. For the moment he was a prosperous farmer, contentedly sipping a steaming mug of *cril* and enjoying the quiet pleasures of an evening at home in his magnificent old farm mansion. Other moments, other identities, and not even Leblanc could have said for certain which one was himself.

But this moment he was a farmer. When he said mildly, 'We've had a rather hectic time here, Supervisor,' he could have been commenting on a prosaic agricultural crisis.

Forzon risked a sip of his own *cril*. It had a delightfully pungent aroma of burnt spices, and it was hot enough to sear his mouth. He set it aside and remarked caustically, 'Likewise.'

Leblanc smiled. Usually Forzon enjoyed analyzing faces, but a brief study of Leblanc's left him in a state of utter frustration. It possessed a disconcerting mobility – plasticity, even – of expression. Coupled with Leblanc's slender, fine-boned stature it gave him an aspect of being constantly in a state of transformation.

'Ann was a bit impetuous,' Leblanc conceded.

'I could think of a stronger word for it.'

'Impetuous,' Leblanc said firmly. 'I reprimanded her, but not severely. Naturally she was upset about this. Members of Team B don't normally mishandle their assignments. If they did there would be no Team B. We mishandled this one, and I'm as much to blame as anyone else, but we don't brood over them, especially when they have happy endings. I assumed that you'd be on your way to one of King Rovva's delightful little entertainments, and when I heard that you were safe and dashed back here to

53

congratulate those who rescued you, they informed me that you had rescued them. I can sympathize with Ann. It wasn't merely strange, it was incredible.'

'Locking me up seemed like a strange way for them to express their gratitude.'

'They didn't actually lock you up,' Leblanc protested. 'I understand your resentment, but you can't have any idea how impossible this seems. Rastadt gave you the Larnorian language, dressed you as a Larnorian priest, and even outfitted you with the most extreme form of Larnorian nose, all of which was maliciously contrived to make you as conspicuous as a horse in a flock of sheep – which is an old Kurrian saying, except that Kurrian horses aren't horses and their sheep are even less like sheep, but it will do. To the Kurrian peasant a Larnorian priest is—'

'I know. *Now* I know. A bogyman.'

'Worse than that. A devil with the direct mission of dragging him into whatever his imagination construes as a nether region. Long ago the priests of Larnor tried to perform missionary work in Kurr. The kings of Kurr did not react kindly to having their religious prerogatives usurped by competitors, and they laid a firm foundation for a vivid folklore concerning the iniquity of Larnorian priests. With that costume, and that language, and that nose, you were doomed the moment you set foot here.'

'I know that,' Forzon said. 'What I don't understand is why Rastadt wanted me doomed. I also don't understand why your Ann Cory, B627, practically invited me into the trap when she could have warned me about it.'

'There were two traps,' Leblanc said. 'The one Rastadt was arranging for you and the one we were arranging for Rastadt. If she'd told you about the one, then Rastadt would have avoided the other – and there was considerable danger that he would find a quicker and more efficient means of getting rid of you. Rastadt – but tonight I'd rather not talk about Rastadt. You're safe. You saved the life of a promising young agent and perhaps saved Ann from being tortured and maimed, and when she gets over the ignominy of being rescued by a CS man she'll thank you. The wine is mulling – this region produces the best wine in Kurr – so let's talk of pleasanter things and leave Rastadt to the cold light of day.'

'I'd rather talk about him now. What happened to him?'

'He just sent me a message.'

'Then – he wasn't captured?'

'I presume not. The message came from base.'

'He said the plane would return for him the next night. Last night. I'm losing track of time.'

Leblanc's face formed a tight, icy smile. 'His message didn't mention his own visit to Kurr. It asked why Team B had not acknowledged the order to meet Supervisor Jef Forzon on his landing the night before last at coordinates N457-W614, and it requested confirmation that contact had been made as ordered. No such order was received.'

'Ah! So that's why no one was there to meet us.'

'I'll go one step further. No such order was sent.'

'The more I know about this,' Forzon said slowly, 'the more confused I feel. Rastadt was dressed like me. He was wearing the Larnorian nose. Why would he set a trap for me and then walk into it himself?'

'It's a long story. Sure you wouldn't rather wait until tomorrow? Well—' He drained his mug and pushed it aside. 'For four hundred years we've been trying to convert Kurr to a democracy. During that time Gurnil has had some highly competent coordinators and one or two shockingly incompetent ones. All of them failed. Seven years ago Rastadt received the Gurnil command. He had an excellent record and a reputation as a resourceful trouble-shooter. He immediately undertook a number of reckless measures, and when his plans didn't work he accused Team B of not carrying out his orders. He then began sending in improperly trained agents of his own selection. He set up virtually an independent command within Team B, and the result was almost disastrous. To put it bluntly, he came very close to blowing the planet. Do you know what that would have meant?'

'Not exactly.'

'IPR would have had to withdraw completely, washing out four hundred years of work. This is the one worst thing that can happen – the thing all IPR officers have nightmares about. Once a native population becomes aware of our presence we have to leave. We can't return until the natives have forgotten we were there, and that may take a millennium or more. If an idea gets translated into superstition and folklore it can go on forever. Rastadt came within a whisker of blowing Gurnil, and having put Team B in the greatest crisis in its history he wouldn't even come here to see us through it. His assistant saved us. From what I know of Rastadt, he probably never thanked the man.'

'Was that Assistant-Coordinator Wheeler?'

Leblanc nodded.

'He said he was a former member of Team B.'

'He did a job for us. We had twenty agents in the hands of King Rovva's congenial torture squads, and between them they knew enough to compromise the whole team. Wheeler rescued all of them.'

'He doesn't look like the heroic type.'

'In that kind of situation resourcefulness counts for more than heroics. He bribed and bluffed and tricked and maybe worked a little magic on the side, but he rescued everyone. Then he persuaded Rastadt to remove his novices and let Team B handle Kurr, which achievement I consider equally astonishing. Since then Rastadt has done nothing at all, and he's kept us from doing anything. Every plan I've submitted has been rejected. For example—'

Forzon raised his hand. 'If you don't mind, let's skip ahead to where I come into this.'

'Of course. A year ago my brother died, leaving some rather complicated family affairs to be straightened out. I took an emergency leave of absence. On my way back I stopped at Supreme Headquarters and read Rastadt's reports. All of them were fraudulent. He described the excellent progress he was making and didn't mention the fiasco that almost cost us the planet. I could have filed charges, but in the eyes of Supreme Headquarters it would have been my word against his until someone got around to an on-the-spot investigation, and those things drag out interminably. And I suspected that more than fraud was involved.

'So I had a frank, off-the-record discussion with an old friend of mine who is First Secretary to the Planning Staff. I convinced him that a high-ranking Cultural Survey officer should be assigned to Gurnil.'

'Why?'

'We need a drastically different approach here. We of the Bureau have our techniques, and they are very good techniques, but obviously they don't work in Kurr. Because of the impressive level of culture it seemed possible that a Cultural Survey officer could help us. I wanted a CS officer of the highest rank compatible with field work, and I wanted him transferred to the Bureau in rank and assigned to Gurnil as Supervising Coordinator. This wasn't an easy thing to arrange, but my friend had the influence to bring it off.'

Forzon said blankly, 'Supervising Coordinator? I was told at base that I was to command Team B.'

Leblanc's voice took on a note of embarrassment. 'I told you we'd set a trap for Rastadt, Supervisor. My apologies, but – you were the bait. As Supervising Coordinator it wouldn't have taken even a Cultural Survey officer long to find out that something is very wrong with the IPR setup on this planet, and Rastadt knew that. As soon as he learned that you'd arrived without orders and didn't know your assignment, he forged orders for you. Then he arranged to land you in a remote part of Kurr without Team B's knowledge and with a language and appearance that guaranteed your immediate capture. Right now he'll be drafting a sad report for Supreme Headquarters, telling how you insisted on visiting Kurr alone and without proper indoctrination and warning Headquarters to never again entrust a Bureau assignment to a CS man.'

'He didn't want me to come,' Forzon said. 'He said it wasn't safe.'

'Naturally he'd put on a good act – make you insist in front of witnesses.'

'But he came with me! Wheeler wanted the job, but Rastadt insisted on coming himself.'

'I'm glad to hear that. Wheeler is a good man, but an assistant is in a damnably awkward position when his superior goes bad. I think Wheeler does the best he can, and my guess is that he intended to see that you reached us safely. Rastadt suspected that and decided to escort you himself.'

'He escorted me,' Forzon said slowly, 'and he walked into that ambush with me.'

'And then he walked right out again. Listen. We didn't use you for bait without taking every possible precaution. I've been sending agents back to base on one pretext or another, one at a time, so I'd have someone there when you arrived. As soon as Ann learned that you'd been given phony orders and the Larnorian language and costume we knew what Rastadt intended to do. The night before you came to Kurr he sent a plane over. We had a beam on it, and we thought it was picking out a suitably remote landing place for you. We had a party waiting there, and the plane came in right on schedule but didn't land. While it was occupying our attention Rastadt sneaked your plane over at low altitude and landed you far to the south. The place was buzzing with soldiers and ruffs – a sinister kind of security agent – and the only people we had in position to help you were picked up almost at once. This means only one thing: Somehow Rastadt is in direct communication with King Rovva, he notified the king that you were coming, and then – probably to forestall Wheeler – he personally led you into the trap. The plane returned the same night to pick him up. You've given us our proof, Supervisor. Rastadt is guilty not just of fraud, but of treason.'

'What could he possibly gain?' Forzon demanded.

Leblanc shook his head. 'I don't know. The man must be insane.'

'What are you going to do about it?'

'Nothing. Rastadt controls the interspatial communications. If I addressed a complaint to Supreme Headquarters it wouldn't be sent. Whatever he's trying to do, he has most of the base personnel in it with him. He'd have to. If I could get in touch with Wheeler I might be able to persuade him to smuggle out a message, but as you've noticed, Rastadt is keeping Wheeler away from Kurr.'

'I'm Supervising Coordinator, you say. What should I do about it?'

'Nothing. You've already accomplished the first task I had in mind for you. I needed proof about Rastadt, and now I have it. The next planetary inspection is only two years away, and that will finish him. I'll wait until he's had plenty of time to file his report, and then I'll advise him that you've arrived safely. It'll be interesting to see how he reacts.

'In the meantime, you *are* Supervising Coordinator, which means that you're my superior and Team B is at your disposal. I hope you'll be able to work out that drastically different approach that we need. Any culturally slanted ideas you can come up with, Team B will be glad to try them out.' He paused to refill his mug. 'CS men are considerably more resourceful than I would have thought possible,' he said thoughtfully. 'No offense intended – batting about on a strange world isn't childplay, even when one is trained for it. Under the circumstances I'd have estimated your likely freedom at something under ten minutes, and yet you turned up the following night to rescue two of my agents and made a flawless job of that, too. How *did* you do it?'

'He doesn't know himself,' Ann Cory said dryly.

Forzon had not heard her come in; he resisted the temptation to glare at her. 'I was able to do it because I met a woman who loved beautiful things, as I do. I didn't understand her language, but beauty has a language of its own. We both understood it. Are the people of that region unusually poor?'

'It's the most impoverished district of Kurr,' Leblanc said. 'I suspect that centuries ago it thrived on smuggling, but after the Larnorian revolution the kings of Kurr went to considerable length to cut off all contact with Larnor. The people had to fall back on agriculture, and the soil there is poor.'

'The smuggling would account for my hiding place. Anyway, this woman was starved for beauty the way a person can be starved for food. She hid me, I think, because if she'd turned me over to the soldiers she'd have had to give up my robe. Whatever the danger, beauty is such a rare thing in her life that she accepts the risk. She knows a language that you don't understand.'

Leblanc said good-naturedly, 'I've lived in Kurr for thirty years, Supervisor. I've studied Kurr and its people as intensely as you've ever studied – well, beauty. If there's any language that the people of Kurr understand and I don't, I'll be very much surprised.'

Forzon seized a taper and marched to the far end of the long room with Ann and Leblanc trailing after him. Paintings leaped to life as the light struck them, rows of paintings, hung from floor to ceiling. 'Are you a connoisseur of art?' Forzon asked.

'No more than is the head of every household in Kurr,' Leblanc said. 'These things aren't *art*. They're just an album of honorable ancestors and familiar scenes, and every home has one.'

'Even in the impoverished south,' Forzon mused.

'Of course, except that the poorer household will have fewer paintings, and they'll be painted by less competent artists who are willing to accept lower fees.'

'That's interesting. Reassuring, I should say,' Forzon said, moving the taper about. 'Kurrian art hasn't declined, just that one family's financial status. The ancestors were able to afford better artists.'

'None of these are actually *my* ancestors, though this peninsula was farmed by another Team B agent before me, and another before him. But if the owner of a farm as prosperous as this one didn't have an extensive family album on display he'd be thought odd. Team B agents survive by never doing anything odd.'

'I suppose the landscapes are views of your farm?'

'Of course. Why would a Kurrian farmer want views of anyone else's farm? Wandering artists stop by every few days, looking for commissions. I have a new scene painted each year, and if I find a portrait among their work samples that looks a little like one of my pseudo ancestors I buy it and hang it up as another relative.'

'That's a dangerous thing to do.'

'I don't think so. Any Kurrian would do the same if he recognized the portrait of a relative among an artist's samples.'

'It's a dangerous thing for *you* to do. Have you had your own portrait painted? Yes, I see it. The artist caught your character. Craftily domineering. Why did you choose that particular artist?'

'I liked his work.'

'Do you have many native visitors?'

'No. I give an annual fete, which is expected of me, but otherwise I have no visitors at all. I play the part of a convivial fellow in the village, and no one thinks it unusual if a bachelor doesn't entertain at home. That's fortunate, because it wouldn't be safe to have neighbors dropping in unexpectedly when I have agents coming and going all the time. The Kurrian peasant isn't much given to socializing anyway, except at harvest fetes.'

'Does your fete take place out of doors?'

'Yes.'

'You're more fortunate than you realize. One glance at this family album, and any astute Kurrian would commence thinking you were odd.'

Leblanc took the taper and backed away slowly, gazing perplexedly at the paintings. Ann kept her eyes on Forzon.

'What's wrong with my family album?' Leblanc demanded.

'I insist that the natives of Kurr display paintings primarily because they love art and enjoy looking at it, and no lover of art would place his cherished collection in this corner. The light is terrible. You don't even have taper brackets here, and in the day-time the only decent light is at the other end of the room. You might as well hang it in a closet.'

'Originally it was at the other end of the room, but years ago I got tired of seeing it there. Do you really think—'

'I do,' Forzon said firmly. 'There's another thing. A private art collection will usually reveal the owner's preferences in art. Your collection reflects such vagaries of taste as to suggest that you have none, which of course you don't. If you actually like your art as staidly conservative as that portrait of yours, you shouldn't be able to tolerate anything as fanciful as the portrait that hangs next to it, or those landscapes on the far right. I see five distinct styles here, and I have the feeling that the native who admires any one of them would have to loathe at least two of the others.' He turned to Ann. 'Tell me this. Have you ever seen more than three of these styles on display in one collection?'

'I've never paid any attention to styles,' she confessed. 'There are five villages that produce all of the artists in Kurr, so it makes sense that there would be five styles, but I've never thought about anyone liking one and not liking another. To me they're all just, well, paintings.'

'Have you had this paint chemically analyzed?' Forzon asked Leblanc.

He said apologetically, 'No—'

'Have you had any *torril* music recorded for study?'

'I never thought it necessary. If anyone wanted to study it, he could hear as much as he cared to listen to.'

'Is there a song literature?'

'The natives sing, yes, but—'

'But you've never paid any attention to it,' Forzon said resignedly. 'It's rare to find an entire people with a natural passion for beauty, but the Kurrians seem to have one. I suppose those benches are ordinary household furnishings, but they're beautiful. Look how carefully the work was laid out to make maximum effectiveness of the wood grain. The same general pattern was used for all of them, but each is an individual creation. The person who crafted them was as much an artist as the person who painted your portrait. Do you mean to say that Team B has lived surrounded by arts and crafts of this quality for four hundred years without noticing them?'

Leblanc did not answer.

Forzon took the taper and stooped to examine the stonework of the floor. No two pieces were the same size and shape, and yet the mason had fitted them flawlessly and contrived exquisite patterns. He turned his attention to a table, whose spiraling legs produced a delightful illusion of height, and then lifted his eyes in admiration at the lovely simplicity of the nulled ceiling beams.

'I'll leave Rastadt to you,' he told Leblanc. 'I wouldn't know what to do about him anyway. Get in touch with Wheeler if you can, or try to get a message out some other way. I gather that the matter isn't urgent. Rastadt can't hurt Team B if you disregard his orders, which you have my permission to do, and, in any case the planetary inspection will settle him. Kurrian affairs have been in a muddle for four hundred years, so another two can't make much difference. As for me – I'll need language lessons. Do you have the equipment?'

'We'll run you through the basic course that all new

Team B agents receive. It takes ten days. What do you propose to do?'

'I meant to set up a cultural survey, but that's out. It's too large a job for one person, and obviously I can expect very little assistance from Team B.'

'We'll give you all the help you want,' Leblanc protested.

Forzon shook his head. 'A cultural survey isn't quite the same thing as an agricultural census. It requires both training and an uncommon aptitude, and your Team B personnel have neither. Ann plays the *torru*, and plays it very well, but how well does she listen? How many styles of *torril* music are there, Ann?'

She did not answer.

'What I propose to do is investigate this Kurrian passion for beauty.'

'Do you think there might be an angle there that we could use to topple King Rovva?' Leblanc asked.

Forzon smiled. 'I haven't the vaguest idea. I'm going to investigate the Kurrian passion for beauty because it interests me.'

SIX

Long before Forzon had mastered the language he was eager to move on. The other agents went about their business, leaving him alone with Leblanc, and though he discovered unexpected beauties in the old farmhouse everywhere he looked, the Team B commander bored him. Leblanc lived surrounded by lovely things and was unaware of them.

The matter of the peasant woman and the robe of the Larnorian priest had disturbed him deeply. 'But why?' he would demand, with a perplexed frown that pushed his normally smooth brow into a mass of wrinkles. 'She

couldn't wear it, or even make it over into other garments!'
Hours later he would turn with a jerk, sloshing mulled
wine over the lips of his bowl, and protest, 'She couldn't
even show it to a friend. The moment it became evident
that she'd been harboring a Larnorian priest she wouldn't
have a friend!'

Forzon exhausted his stock of quotations on the subject
of beauty and fell silent.

Twenty days after his arrival a new Team B agent appeared, a husky, deeply tanned, jovial man named Hance
Ultman. He was a produce dealer, and his occupation enabled him to range freely through Kurr's central districts.

'Do you have room for a passenger?' Forzon asked him.

Ultman flashed his infectious grin. 'If the passenger
doesn't mind walking!'

Leblanc made no objection. Ultman's business was perfectly legitimate, Forzon would be safe with him, and such
a leisurely peregrination would provide an ideal introduction to Kurr and its people.

'Make the rounds, then,' Leblanc said. 'You'll meet
other agents along the way and in Kurra, and perhaps I'll
be able to see you there. Or you can come back here. And
if you think of anything—'

Forzon nodded impatiently. Leblanc had lately seized
upon the notion that the strange Kurrian passion for beauty
might be converted to a passion for democracy, and if
Forzon thought of a way to accomplish that he intended
to keep it to himself.

Two days later they set out. Ultman had six heavy
wagons, each pulled by a pair of placid and obedient *esgs*.
Ultman marched by the lead team; the others were tied to
the wagons ahead of them, starting when they started and
stopping when they stopped. Forzon took his place opposite
Ultman, and they shouted back and forth above the incessant creaking of the wagons.

'Why don't you grease these things?' Forzon demanded.

'The Rule of One,' Ultman shouted cheerfully. 'Which

is really a Rule of Nothing. If I greased the wheels I'd be guilty of introducing a technological innovation. Actually, the Kurrians would have thought of it long ago if this wood weren't so tough that it lasts indefinitely without lubrication.'

'The wood may be tough, but what about their eardrums?'

Ultman grinned and did not answer, and Forzon spent the next hour attempting to reconcile the natives' love for music with their tolerance for noise.

Ultman specialized in a luxury food, a type of tuber that few farmers cultivated. He bought always from the same sources, scattered widely about central Kurr. They moved slowly along narrow country roads, from village to village and farmhouse to farmhouse, and to Forzon it was a journey through wonderland.

They visited an artists' village, which had quaintly square mushroom houses and a scenic, slow-moving river. All of the male children, from toddlers to adolescents, were out in the bright sunshine painting the river, the houses, the countryside, their younger sisters or each other. There were no adult males in evidence; they ranged far throughout most of the year, painting portraits and local scenes for the private galleries that adorned every home in Kurr. Ultman good-naturedly consented to remain in the village long enough for Forzon to have his portrait painted by a youngster whose technique interested him, but the excitement of a first commission so unsettled the youth that the result was mediocre.

The secrets of arts and crafts were jealously guarded and passed along from father to son, and as they followed their slowly spiraling course toward the capital city they encountered a woodcarvers' village, a sculptors' village, even a poets' village, each of them a monument to Kurr's insatiable demand for art and the wealth which the country was willing to lavish upon it.

They visited a musicians' village on a feast day, and the

village street was the setting for dozens of recitals. Forzon moved from group to group, watching entranced as shiny-faced urchins made their first public appearances with small, high-pitched *torrils* that matched their diminutive height, and young men in their late teens gave masterful renditions on full-sized instruments with booming bass tones. Women and children in colorful holiday costume listened intently and applauded with frenzied stomping on the painted paving stones. Forzon drifted about in a giddy intoxication of sheer delight with the shimmering music until he was suddenly stricken with remorse because he had brought no equipment with which to record it.

Ultman, obviously pleased to have someone to talk with, talked incessantly. Much of what he said was blanketed by the infernal creaking of his wagons, but Forzon managed to filter out such information as seemed of value to him. Then Ultman got onto the subject of Team B's failures and rambled on for hours, and Forzon, remembering the roomful of files at base, steeled himself against an impending doom of boredom.

'Women,' Ultman shouted. Forzon nodded, marveling at the man's vocal stamina. 'That was another angle. The Kurrian woman isn't much more than a domestic animal, though a happy, respected, well-treated animal.'

'Is that so?' Forzon shouted back, remembering how the peasant woman had instantly cowed her husband in the matter of the priest's robe. 'I've noticed that they don't take much of a role in the arts.'

Ultman halted the lead team with a swipe of his hand and reached into the wagon for the wine crock. He drank deeply and passed it to Forzon. 'Nor in anything else,' he said, booming his words into the unaccustomed silence. He laughed merrily and lowered his voice. 'A few daughters of musicians teach music to the daughters of the wealthy, but that's all.'

Forzon replaced the crock and turned away, eager to move on, but Ultman was of a mood for talk. He perched on the edge of the wagon as though to compose himself for an oration. 'Team B once worked for years trying to bring about a revolt through an equal rights for women movement and failed to convince any women that they lacked equal rights. Then there was religion. The king is the religion in Kurr. Not exactly a god, but at least an ultra-high priest. Maybe that's why he's so sensitive about missionaries from Larnor – doesn't want others working his side of the street, so to speak. Anyway, dozens of variations have been tried on the religion angle.'

'Has anyone tried a cultural angle?' Forzon asked.

'Someone must have. *Everything* has been tried in Kurr.' He thought for a moment. 'Someone once persuaded a district governor to put a tax on paintings. It only lasted until King Rovva found out about it, and he canceled the tax and sent the governor to a one-hand village. Old Rovva is too smart to be taken in by a taxation gimmick.'

'If the king's habit of dispatching worthy citizens to a one-hand village were properly publicized, his popularity would be bound to suffer. Why don't you establish a newspaper?'

'It couldn't criticize the king, not if it wanted to stay in business. Anyway, printing hasn't been invented.'

'Make Kurr a present of it.'

Ultman laughed uproariously, slapping the side of the wagon until his bewildered beasts were startled into motion. He leaped down to halt them. 'Make Kurr a present of it!' he gasped. 'The Rule of One—'

'Whenever I suggest anything,' Forzon complained, 'someone cites the Rule of One, but no one has bothered to tell me what it is.'

'Centuries ago a bright young agent wanted to help a revolution along by giving the rebels a primitive type of firearm. It was considered a stupid request because the Bureau maintained a strict ban on technological innovations, but contrary to everyone's expectations Supreme

68

Headquarters didn't reject the request out of hand. Instead, the Rule of One was formulated. Bureau agents were permitted to introduce one technological change per world, but only one. That made the young agent happy – until he learned that the *one* was to be taken literally and there were maybe a thousand innovations in the rifle alone, not to mention the cartridges. He was laughed out of the service and since then no one has attempted to use technological assistance. The Rule of One is still on the books, though.'

'Then we could introduce the type, but no printing press. Or the press, but no type.'

'It isn't even that simple. There'd be dozens of innovations in either the press or the type, and probably as many more before you could produce paper in the necessary quantity. But about culture. Your best bet would be to request a review of the records. Those girls at base got nothing to do anyway, and it wouldn't take them long to run the index file through a machine and pick out the references that interest you.' He reached for the wine crock again. 'Leblanc and his mulled wine. I like mine *cold*, and you can't hardly get any that way in Kurr.'

'Wrap some cloth around the crock and keep it soaked with water,' Forzon suggested.

'I can't,' Ultman said sadly. 'I might be guilty of contributing a technological innovation.' He raised his hands despairingly. 'It's the one thing I miss. A cold drink. The dratted winters aren't cold enough to freeze things. I can't remember the last time I saw any ice. Otherwise, it's a real nice place to work.'

He jumped down and slapped the lead team of *esgs* on their flanks. The screeching racket began anew, and Forzon dutifully took his place beside the plodding animals.

It was a lovely land, this country of Kurr, but much of the loveliness was *created*, was the expression of an astonishingly artistic people. They passed fields of grain laid out in geometric patterns, like flowerbeds. One field, high on a hilltop where its shimmering beauty could be seen for miles, was a rippling sea of riotously colored flowers. 'What do they raise the flowers for?' Forzon shouted. 'Honey? Perfume?'

Ultman shook his head. 'They haven't any honey insects. Sugar is processed from the leaves of a sugar bush, and they get their perfume extracts from roots. You see those flowers everywhere, mostly on hilltops. I've often wondered why they don't plow them under and plant something useful.'

'Such as tubers?' Forzon suggested with a smile.

The IPR Bureau would do that, just as it would plow this stable society and happy, prosperous, beauty-loving people with the sharp edge of revolution. Forzon wondered if popular government might not be a form of creative expression, doomed eternally to failure here in Kurr because the people lavished their creative energy upon such impractical matters as art and music and poetry – and fields of flowers.

Like Leblanc, Ultman was not attuned to the beauty that surrounded him. Works of art were things, just as the tubers he dealt in were things, and no doubt had their uses; but he was as unlikely to become emotional over one as the other. What motivated him, then? Team B's mission?

He wasn't greatly concerned about that. He had a job to do and he was doing it – moving about the central districts, maintaining his contacts, carrying messages, collecting information. Dangerous? He couldn't remember the last time Team B lost an agent. Several agents had been in a fix a few years before, but someone had cracked it. Someone always did. Team B's mission was for higher-ups to worry about, and if one of them thought of something Ultman could do to advance it he would say so, and Ultman would do it.

Forzon reflected wryly that anyone interested in solving IPR's problem in Kurr might first have to solve the problem of IPR's Team B. For all their lack of interest in art its members were dramatic artists, more intent on playing their roles correctly than using them to any purpose.

They moved along peaceful, verdant lanes upon which the picturesque villages with their quaint, multi-colored houses were strung like glowing, widely separated beads upon a green thread. From time to time they looked in at a village tavern, a public room in an ordinary private home, and sampled the new crop of wine. There was no such thing as an inn. In this mild and friendly and prosperous land the traveler who carried a heavy cloak wanted for nothing. He slept in the open. Any woman with a pot of food would cheerfully feed hungry strangers, and if the strangers offered one or two tubers in exchange she would serve princely portions and add sweet cakes from the hoard she was accumulating for the next feast day.

Occasionally they encountered Team B agents. Two of them, a tavern owner and his wife, invited Ultman and Forzon to stay overnight and then ruined Forzon's long anticipated reunion with a bed by keeping him awake most of the night with their and Ultman's reminiscences. A wine dealer, a traveling merchant, a wool buyer – they turned up unexpectedly and passed by Ultman's string of wagons without so much as a nod. A farmer Ultman called on to buy tubers. Another farmer who strolled into a tavern where they were drinking, slowly sipped a measure of wine, and departed without exchanging a word with them.

'We didn't have any business,' Ultman said afterward, 'or I'd have arranged to meet with him privately. He came in because he wanted to see you close up. Some day you may be glad that he knows who you are.'

Ultman's six wagons were heaped high with sweet-smelling tubers when they finally reached one of the main roads to Kurra. It was wide enough for two-way traffic, and so heavily traveled with carts and wagons hauling farm produce to the capital city that they waited an hour for a gap wide enough for Ultman's string of wagons. Later that same day, when Kurra was already a massive blur on the

71

horizon, traffic on the road ahead of them came to an abrupt stop, and Ultman hurriedly steered his wagons off the road and halted.

A lone foot traveler approached them. He wore a bright uniform, already travel-stained, and he trudged along wearily with his eyes on the dust that rippled under his feet. People took to the fields to go around him or turned aside and halted until he had passed. The left sleeve of his coat flapped loosely at his side.

'One of the king's grooms,' Ultman whispered. 'He's displeased His Majesty, so now he's on his way to a one-hand village. Until he reaches it he's an outcast. People will feed him, but they won't speak to him, and they won't feed him more than once.'

The one-handed man passed into the distance, and behind him traffic began to move, foot travelers returned to the road, and the land of Kurr was again lovely and serene; but the shadow of his passing hung over Forzon for a long time.

They spent the night with the farmer who cared for Ultman's wagons and *esgs* when Ultman was not using them, and early the next morning they entered the walled city of Kurra with one wagon, pulled by a single *esg*.

'It's the law,' Ultman explained. 'Very sensible, too. Most of King Rovva's laws are. A convoy of six wagons in this place would cause traffic jams you'd have to see to believe. Probably one did, and the king got caught in it, and after he'd sent everyone concerned to a one-hand village he issued a law that would keep it from happening again.'

The old buildings were built – Forzon gaped in amazement – of *stone*, but with the same outward flaring walls seen on wood buildings in the rural areas. Even the high stone wall around the city curved outward at the top. 'I'd like to dismantle one of them and see how they do it,' he told Ultman, who shrugged and said that he liked his walls

72

solid and standing and was content to leave them that way.

The curving roofs of the rural buildings had been set directly atop the flared walls; the stone buildings of Kurra had straight-walled upper stories. These, because of the flared lower walls, extended far out over the winding streets, and above the narrow sidestreets they met to form tunnels. Kurra was a city of tunnels, with only the main thoroughfares open to the sky.

Where the villages had been the homes of artists, the city harbored artisans. Shops of craftsmen and crude hand manufactories lined the streets. A short distance inside the city gate their route took them past a large market place, a riotous melange of colorful costume, piles of foodstuffs, crafted products of all kinds, artists with display panels of their work discussing prices with prospective clients or painting portraits, and at the center of the market, the area most remote from rickety traffic noises, performing *torril* players surrounded by impromptu audiences. There was noise – the cries of vendors, the bickering shouts of their customers, the distant blending of the contiguous *torril* recitals, the sheer, laughing exuberance of a happy people, overlaid with a heavy veneer of creaking from passing carts and wagons.

Deep into the city they paused at a tunneled sidestreet until Ultman had dashed ahead to make certain that a wagon did not enter from the other end and block their way. They made their turn, maneuvered the wagon through a lesser tunnel into a courtyard, and backed it down an earthen ramp to a cellar entrance.

'Home!' Ultman announced.

Forzon helped him to unload, and they returned wagon and *esg* to the farm and brought in another laden wagon. It was evening before the last of the wagons was unloaded and returned to the farm, and they had to sprint to reach the city gate before it closed.

Ultman would hawk his tubers about the tunneled streets and byways of Kurra with a hand cart, and by the time he finally disposed of them a new crop would be ready. He'd been following this same cycle for years. He was known everywhere, he could come and go as he pleased, and if he dropped from sight for a time none of his native contacts thought it unusual. It seemed to Forzon that Ultman had an ideal occupation for a Team B agent, but he did not care for Ultman's gloomy cellar.

Neither did Ultman. 'But it has its advantages,' he said. 'The wise Bureau agent always has an escape route laid out. Even if there's help nearby the other agents have their own lives to lead, and they can't stand around watching just in case you get into trouble. You have to let them know that you need help, which you can't do if you get yourself trapped in living quarters that have only one exit. First thing I do in new quarters is dig an escape tunnel. The one I have here leads to some spare storage bins I rent in the next house. You can't dig tunnels from an upper storey. You have to build passageways, and that takes building materials and is anyway a touchy business. You also have to control the apartment next door, which isn't nearly as simple as renting a corner of a cellar. Me, I'd rather live where I can dig. Now I'll order a meal from my landlady to celebrate my home-coming, and then we'll have a look at Kurr's night life.'

Night *death*, Forzon thought, when they set out through the darkened streets. The enclosing buildings intensified the gloom; there was no vehicular traffic, and the resultant, uncanny silence produced an atmosphere as tense as it was funereal. The light of tapers showed dimly in a few unshuttered upper windows, but this was small help to pedestrians in the cavernous streets below.

At infrequent intervals a torch burned in a bracket high above the heads of the passerby. 'Taverns,' Ultman explained. 'They have to keep a torch burning as long as they're open. Shall we try one?'

They marched down a long stone ramp to a cellar entrance. The proprietor, or *pourer*, let out a shout when he

74

saw Ultman and sprang forward to greet them. He gave Ultman a hefty nudge, the Kurrian handshake. Ultman belted him one in return, they both laughed, and Ultman remarked that they had time for a glass or two. That startled Forzon; he'd seen no glass drinking vessels in Kurr.

The glasses were a timing device, hemispheres of clear glass set in a wood frame, their lower ends drawn into spouts. They seated themselves at a round table inset with a deep bowl of liquid. The pourer ladled their glasses full of liquid; it slowly bubbled out into the central bowl, and they were free to drink until their glasses were empty.

They filled their own drinking bowls, and Forzon took a cautious sip and masked his grimace. It was an extremely bitter beer.

'I didn't think you'd like it,' Ultman said, 'but you should sample everything, if only for your own protection. Otherwise you might get into a situation where you'd have to spend an evening drinking the stuff.'

'Do you like it?'

Ultman shrugged. 'I'm used to it.'

He struck up a conversation with a man at the next table, another produce dealer. Forzon began to study his surroundings. Unlike Ultman's damp hole, this cellar was lavishly finished. Pillars of hewn logs supported huge lintels, which in turn held up the smaller ceiling beams. Forzon quickly assured himself that the building was in no danger of collapse, but he felt less certain about the economic structure of city tavern keeping. A few fast drinkers could bankrupt a pourer in an evening.

But these patrons were not drinkers. They sipped infrequently while they talked, or, if they were alone, gazed hypnotically at their bubbling glasses or at the flickering reflections of wall tapers in the deep pools of beer and wine. The pourer prowled relentlessly, ready to pounce the moment a glass bubbled empty. He would tap the customer on the shoulder; the customer would drain his bowl with a gulp, stare resentfully at the pourer, and then pay for another glass or depart.

A *torril* player entered, panting from the descent with his heavy instrument. He played a short number, looked about hopefully, shouldered his *torril* again.

'No one paid him,' Ultman explained.

'*I'll* pay him,' Forzon said, starting to get to his feet.

'Better not. He can't be very good, or the pourer would offer him a glass.'

An artist wandered through with an armful of samples, making appointments for the next day. Another *torril* player came in. Someone tossed him a small coin when he finished; he scornfully tossed it back and left. Their glasses emptied for the third time, and Ultman jerked his head at the door.

A short distance further on the street opened onto another, a wider street, that blazed with torches in both directions. 'The Avenue of Taverns,' Ultman explained. 'You'll find them all over the city, but there are more here than anywhere else. Shall we try another?'

They tried four in rapid succession, sampling a dozen varieties of wine and beer. *Torril* players came and went; finally one, obviously an artist, remained, playing number after number to a shower of coins. When he paused to rest Forzon found himself seated near a congenial group that was arguing the virtues of various *torril* celebrities. He listened delightedly, and then found to his disgust that Ultman had chanced upon another produce dealer and was discussing – tubers. The *torril* player returned to his instrument and played until the outside torch burned out, when the pourer stoutly resisted all importunities to light another and evicted them.

Most of the taverns were closed, and they fumbled their way back to Ultman's cellar in almost total darkness, Forzon uncertain as to whether his lightheadedness derived from the wine or the *torril* music.

'When we started out tonight I thought you were taking

76

me to meet someone from Team B,' he remarked, as they felt their way down Ultman's ramp.

Ultman halted. 'Who did you think you were with all evening? You met at least a dozen Team B agents.'

'Oh,' Forzon said, abashed.

'Some of the higher-ups want a talk with you, but there's no hurry. They probably want to know if you've picked up any ideas.'

Forzon chuckled. 'About converting Kurr to a democracy?'

'I suppose. It's their job to worry about things like that. But then – you're a sector supervisor, so I suppose it's your job to worry about them, too.'

Forzon had never looked upon responsibility in quite that way – as an obligation to worry. He fell asleep much less easily than he had expected.

SEVEN

Tubers falling into Ultman's hand cart with drum-like thuds awakened Forzon at dawn. He clutched his throbbing head and moaned, 'Must you?'

'Got to do what looks natural,' Ultman remarked, with ghastly cheerfulness. 'A produce dealer just back with a fresh stock doesn't loaf around until the stuff starts to rot. Got to see all my best customers this morning.'

Forzon turned over resentfully and covered his ears. Ultman loaded his cart, smoked up the poorly ventilated room brewing himself a mug of *cril*, and finally, with a blunt suggestion that Forzon remain out of sight until he returned, creaked his way up the ramp and was gone.

Forzon had no intention of being seen by anyone. Later he might want to contemplate this notion that a Team B agent's normal routine could not be varied an iota even to accommodate a sector supervisor with a hangover, but for the moment he was content to envelop himself in a cool shroud of silence and try to sleep. He dozed off thinking that the camouflaged entrance to the escape tunnel was only an arm's length away and he'd never have time to use it. There was no lock on the door, and if the king's ruffs burst in on him he'd be a captive before he was fully awake. Even if he miraculously gained the tunnel he wouldn't know where to go once he reached the other end.

When next he awoke Ultman had returned with a hot meat cake, the headache had vanished, and the day, even in the depths of Ultman's cellar, looked immeasurably brighter.

'Got some news,' Ultman exulted. 'The king has ordered a festival for tonight.'

'What sort of festival?'

'A public entertainment. Singing, dancing, music – the works. Any male citizen with the price of admission is welcome. The king commandeers the best entertainers available, the audience has a good time, and I'd guess that His Majesty makes a tidy profit. Want to go?'

'I wouldn't even consider not going,' Forzon said gravely.

'We'll go, then. While you're eating I'll give you some pointers on how to behave in the streets of Kurra.'

'Did you see all of your best customers?'

'Enough of them,' Ultman said with a grin. 'In this business, that's the secret of success. If you do the expected thing enough of the time, people just naturally assume that you're doing it all of the time.'

They spent the afternoon walking the tunneled streets of Kurra and browsing in small shops whenever Forzon saw anything of interest. They bought nothing, though when Forzon became fascinated with a beautifully engraved silver drinking bowl Ultman had a glorious bargaining session with the silversmith, first over the price in raw silver, and then in copper coins, and finally, when the purchase seemed settled, over the weight of tubers that the smith would accept in barter. Passersby stopped to listen delightedly or to join in the bargaining, and abruptly an auction developed, with bystanders bidding up the price that Ultman's vigorous haggling had beaten down. The bowl was carried off by a well-dressed stranger who made only one bid – the last.

The smith offered another bowl, but Forzon thought it inferior to the first, and they moved on.

'That sort of thing is a bit in your line, isn't it?' Ultman asked. On the daytime streets of Kurra they could speak Galactic in relative security. Against the background of screeching carts and wagons, hawking peddlers, and bargaining shoppers there was small danger of being overheard. They had difficulty in hearing each other. Ultman said seriously, 'Would you like to run a shop like that?'

'I don't think so.'

'Well, keep your eyes open for things that interest you. You'll need several occupations.'

'*Several?*'

'Right. If there's a blowup it gives you a place to run.'

'How can you have several occupations simultaneously?'

'All it takes is a little planning. I buy and peddle tubers, but I also help out in a tavern on the other side of town. Sometimes I sleep there for a few nights, do whatever the pourer wants done, take whatever he offers me. The important thing is that I'm known there, and I can turn up unexpectedly any time and be welcome. Then a couple of Team B agents who run businesses have me entered as an assistant, and I put in time there every now and then so their customers will know me. Of course I have a different identity for each place.'

'You people don't leave much to chance.'

Ultman flashed his grin. 'Like Leblanc says, any time a Team B agent starts feeling secure, he's in danger.'

'How safe am I as your assistant?'

'Not very safe. Produce dealers don't normally have

79

assistants, and while the rural people won't pay much attention to your traveling with me once – you might be someone who happened to be going in the same direction – they'd get curious if you were still with me on the next trip. No one's going to be very interested if you share my cellar here in Kurra, but if you hang around long without visible means of support some of my neighbors will commence wondering about you, and in Kurra no one wonders about anything for very long before the king's ruffs start wondering, too.'

'I don't suppose there's an art museum that could use a curator.'

Ultman chuckled. 'I don't suppose so.'

'Thus far I haven't seen a job that I'd care for, but I'll keep looking. Let's have a drink.'

Ultman said sternly, 'No decent Kurrian drinks before sunset. Not in Kurra. Not in public, anyway. The taverns don't open until it's dark enough to justify lighting a torch.'

'Is that another of King Rovva's sensible laws?' Forzon asked, with the aggrieved tone of a man with a thirst.

'It keeps the citizens soberly at work.'

'It also saves the king the cost of street lighting. I take back everything I said. The Kurrians have ample reason to revolt, and the sooner the better.'

They walked as far as the center of the city, where the king's castle sat like a massive stone mushroom in the center of an open square. Above the main entrance the festival proclamation hung unfurled, its message painted in huge letters. When finally they returned to Ultman's cellar they found that someone had left a package – the engraved drinking bowl.

Forzon said bewilderedly, 'You mean – the person who bought it was—'

'Team B. Of course. It wouldn't do for peddlers like us to be buying such things, and he thought you wanted it. It's all right for a peddler to try and bargain, but if the bidding starts he's wise to back out, especially if the ruffs are about, and they were. They might decide to wonder how a peddler came to be having so much money. It wouldn't be a good idea to leave this laying around here, either. On the way to the festival I'll take it to Lweyn and tell him to put it in the hole for you until you have a place of your own.'

At dusk they took their places in line, and to the accompaniment of clinking coins passed through special gates in the city wall and entered the royal amphitheater. Long, curving stone tiers had been built into the steep slope of a natural depression. At the bottom, in the center of an arena, stood a small, many-windowed mushroom-shaped house.

'The king's private box,' Ultman whispered.

They took their seats at the rear – Ultman muttering that it wasn't a good idea to have too many people between them and the exit – and watched the place fill up with people. The slowly settling darkness obliterated even the shadowy shapes of their neighbors, but spectators continued to arrive and stumble about in search of seats. Finally the king and his entourage marched in a stately procession of torches down the slope to the house. Torches were lit around the circular arena, and the performance began.

Momentarily Forzon's interest centered on the king, but at such a distance, and in the flickering torchlight, he could make out nothing except a bulky, robed figure when one of the royal spectators leaned forward. Frustrated, he turned his attention to the entertainment.

At first impression it seemed chaotic. At each side of the arena an artist was at work on a huge canvas. 'The king awards a prize to the one he likes best,' Ultman explained. A poet was reciting his latest opus; the acoustics were flawless, but many of the figurative allusions were lost on Forzon. A troop of dancers circled the arena, moving with a heavy-footed, slow motion but weaving their bodies in fantastic gyrations. A block of soldiers stood in tight for-

81

mation, apparently doing nothing at all, but as Forzon watched them their inner lines shifted slowly and assumed the shape of a flower bud that expanded and began to unfold its petals. The flower vanished in a series of slowly changing geometric designs.

Abruptly the stage was cleared of all except the artists. A uniformed attendant carried in a beautifully carved and inlaid *torril*, and the audience, which had maintained an attitude of respectful silence up to that point, greeted the musician with a thunder of stomping applause.

'They call him Tor,' Ultman whispered, when the noise had subsided. 'Meaning that he's practically synonymous with his instrument. He's the best, and he's a relatively young man.'

Tor seated himself facing the *torril* and encircled the strings with his hands. Watching intently, Forzon made a discovery. The height of a *torril* matched the musician's height, but the size of the globular sounding medium matched his skill. The larger the globe, the greater the number of strings that could be attached to its circumference, and the greater the instrument's range and its demands on the performer.

Tor's instrument had an enormous globe, and the tone, from the booming bass strings to the bell-like trebles, possessed an enriched resonance that made the simple instruments played in taverns sound like toys by comparison. With hands that scarcely seemed to move he brought forth notes with unbelievable rapidity. The music sang joyfully, sank to a muted lament, whispered of songful beauty, and crescendoed to a brilliantly martial conclusion. The audience sprang to its feet to stomp and cheer, Forzon with it.

'I've never heard anything like that,' he confided to Ultman, when the tumult had died down.

Tor was beginning another number. The rippling, surging onslaught on the strings commenced low and gradually moved through the whole range of the instrument in looping patterns of sound. It halted with such shattering suddenness that the ear disbelieved and trustfully searched the silence for the vanished music.

Tor got to his feet and stood facing the house's central window, head bowed. One robe-bedecked figure had leaned forward; obviously the king was speaking, though his words did not carry to the audience.

Forzon held his breath until he had to gasp for air. Ultman's shadowed face seemed set in bewilderment. Amidst a silence that was deathlike, the watching thousands simply watched.

Guards surrounded Tor and stripped him bare to the waist. Then, because it happened so quickly, it was over before Forzon fully grasped the horror of it – the flashing sword, the shriek of pain, a doctor working on the blood-spurting stump of an arm. Forzon did not realize he was on his feet until Ultman roughly hauled him back, whispering frantically, 'Careful, careful—'

The crowd sat as though hypnotized by its own silence as Tor, his arm bandaged, his clothing restored, staggered away. The attendant removed the *torril,* and where great music had welled up a moment before there remained only the blood-stained dust and the fragment of a man's arm. The arm lay untouched through the remainder of the festival, the performers avoiding it nervously.

'Why?' Forzon choked. 'Why? He was a great musician.'

Ultman motioned for silence. 'He *was,*' he whispered bluntly.

There was impressive singing, dancers who performed spectacularly to the beat of small drums, acrobats playing a complicated game that involved the tossing of lighted torches about the darkened arena, tinkling bells, deep-throated gongs, more poetry, singing, dancing – all of it should have fascinated, but Forzon's benumbed mind refused to concentrate. He felt violently ill. He wanted to leave, but he knew without asking that to leave the king's festival before its finale might have fateful consequences.

The crowd had been stunned out of its enthusiasm; the

entertainers moved as though pursued by terror. The thing dragged on for another ghastly hour before the king and his entourage finally departed, and the crowd was free to slowly file out.

Ultman did not speak until they had turned into a tunneled sidestreet and left the crowd behind them. 'They say it happens all the time,' he remarked thoughtfully, 'but I've never heard of it being done in public, and not even in private to a popular figure like Tor. Old Rovva must be having fits about something. Maybe he has another toothache. His last is said to have resulted in a fifty per cent turnover in the royal services.'

The image of that severed limb burned painfully in Forzon's memory. He said soberly, 'That man would have been considered a great artist anywhere.'

'He was more than that. These musicians travel around a lot, and Tor was the best. I suppose you'd call him a national hero. The king must have been out of his mind.'

They threaded their way through the involved pattern of dark, winding streets, Forzon mutely following Ultman's lead and wondering if he could possibly have found his way back to the cellar by himself. There were few taverns in that part of the city, and the only light was an occasional glint seeping through a shuttered window. In the darkness everything looked different to Forzon, and it was not until they had walked much farther than seemed necessary that he realized that everything *was* different.

'We're going a different way, aren't we?' he asked.

'Yes,' Ultman said shortly.

They reached an open space formed by the intersection of several streets. A tavern torch burned on the far side. Ultman drew Forzon back into the shadows and whispered, 'See that window?'

Forzon sighted into the darkness, leaning forward to look past the building's veering overhang. 'I'm not sure—'

'In the daytime there are flowers in that window. At night there's a light.'

'There isn't any light,' Forzon objected.

'That's the idea.'

They hurried on, and Forzon suddenly realized that Ultman was repeatedly glancing behind him. 'We have signs like that all over Kurra,' he said. 'We make it a habit to check them whenever possible. That's the third window tonight that's supposed to have a light but doesn't. It means that Team B is in trouble.'

'What do we do?'

'I don't know yet.'

'Cultural Survey was never like this,' Forzon muttered. He began to watch the passing pedestrians uneasily.

They walked for some distance, keeping to the shadows as much as possible, and then Ultman halted under a tavern's torch while he deliberately removed his cloak and folded it over his arm. A moment later a stooped old hag of a woman came out of a doorway and hobbled toward them. She leered at Forzon, exchanged a few pungent remarks with Ultman, and, as she passed them, hissed, 'Storm three'.

She disappeared around a corner; they took the opposite direction, and after a long, wearying walk Ultman led Forzon down the ramp of a shabby tavern. The few customers eyed them indifferently and decided to ignore them. They took the most remote table and laid out their coins, and as the fat pourer filled their glasses he whispered softly, 'There's been a big cave-in, but I don't think they got anyone.'

'Need any help?' Ultman whispered back.

'I don't think so. My group is clean so far. Have your drinks, and then check in upstairs. I'll spread the word that you're here. Everyone has been looking for you.'

Ultman calmly splashed beer into his drinking bowl. Forzon glanced about the room apprehensively, but no one seemed to be paying any attention to them.

'Joe's a good man,' Ultman said. 'Drink some beer. The old woman is pretty good, too. Did you recognize her?'

Forzon filled his bowl, sipped the beer, concealed his grimace by drawing his hands across his mouth. 'No. Should I have recognized her?'

'I thought you knew her. Ann Cory. She usually goes about as an old dame in Kurra. It isn't safe for a girl to be young and attractive around old Rovva's court. Drink some more beer.'

Forzon did, wondering if the IPR field manual had anything to say about patience. About dawdling over a bowl of beer in a tavern when your life was in danger, just because it would be conspicuous to leave quickly. He regarded Ultman with new respect; at the same time he felt that one glass would have been sufficient proof of normality, but Ultman, after deliberating the matter, indifferently produced more coins and announced that he'd have another.

Eyes converged on them when they got up to leave, followed them to the door, turned away. The pourer moved off to attend to an empty glass. They climbed the ramp and boldly entered the building by its street door, and inside a husky guard grinned at them, shook Ultman's hand, and jerked his head at the stairs. In an upstairs room they found an elderly man in faded robes seated at a table beside a wine crock. He scrutinized Forzon through blindly staring, watery eyes that were masked with cataracts and told him to make himself at home.

'How bad is it?' Ultman asked.

'Your group is blown. There's a watch on your house. We were covering all the approaches so you wouldn't walk into it.'

'I always check,' Ultman said dryly.

The old man shrugged. '*You* we weren't worried about. As for how bad it is, the commander is on his way, and that means it couldn't be much worse.'

'Paul? Coming here?'

'By plane,' the old man said softly. 'And you know that Paul Leblanc wouldn't be flying to Kurra or anywhere else inland, even by night, if it weren't too late to matter.

There's only one possible explanation: our officious co-ordinator has meddled once too often and blown the planet. The only thing left to be done is to get everyone out – and fast.'

EIGHT

'I'm Sev Rawner,' the old man said. 'Gurnil B318. Sit down, Supervisor. You need a drink.' He filled a drinking bowl with a steady hand and eye that belied his age and apparent blindness.

'I just had a drink,' Forzon protested.

'You don't get drink like this in a tavern. Try it.'

Forzon tasted cautiously, and then took a long, savoring draught. 'What is it?'

'The forbidden elixir,' Rawner said with a grin. 'It's a whiskey made from the seeds of the *wulnn*, which is a Kurrian tree, and you're guaranteed a one-way trip to a one-hand village if you're caught with any in your possession.'

'Why should the king object to whiskey?'

'He doesn't. He has a private cellar that would make him the envy of any world in this sector. He just objects to his subjects drinking it. Wants a sober, hard-working citizenry, I suppose. Or maybe he wants to keep the whole crop for himself.'

Forzon raised his bowl again. 'This stuff is forbidden – and you haven't been able to incite a revolution?'

'It's rare. The average citizen couldn't afford it even if it were legal. The supply of *wulnn* trees is limited.'

'Plant more trees.'

'It takes forty years to grow a tree to a seed-producing age.'

'Team B has plenty of time.'

'No.' Rawner shook his head sadly. 'Team B's time has run out. You can't create a demand for a product until you put enough of it in circulation for people to know what it is. There'll never be enough of this whiskey to do that; whenever the king's ruffs find a *wulnn* tree growing outside the royal preserves they cut it down. Enjoy your drink and look for something else to start a revolution. Do you need anything, Hance?'

Ultman poured himself a bowl of the whiskey and downed it slowly. '*Now* I don't need anything.'

'Money?' Rawner tossed a bag of coins onto the table, and Ultman helped himself.

'What about the supervisor?' Ultman asked.

'We'll look after him.'

'Let me know when. See you around, Supervisor.' Ultman shook Forzon's hand, opened a wall panel, and disappeared into the dark passageway beyond. The panel closed silently.

'We'll all be moving on very shortly,' Rawner said. 'Joe thinks his group is clean, but I'm afraid it's just because the ruffs haven't worked out this far. How does it feel to be wanted?'

'It's a new experience. I suppose this is old stuff to you.'

'No. Definitely not old stuff. King Rovva has always been on the alert for subversive elements, but this time he is definitely after Team B. *And King Rovva is not supposed to know that there is a Team B.* What do you think of this?'

He held up a small painting – a portrait of Jef Forzon.

Forzon eyed it critically. 'As an example of the painter's craft, very little. It's rather crudely done. The perspective is deplorable.'

'It's an adequate likeness, though,' Rawner observed, holding it up to the light and squinting at it thoughtfully. 'The crudeness is to be expected when an artist has to copy at top speed from an unfamiliar medium. Don't you recognize it?'

'My ID photo!' Forzon exclaimed. 'Where did you get this?'

'A ruff was making inquiries with it. King Rovva probably has half the artists in Kurra turning these out, but this is the first we've seen. *A Bureau identification photo* —' He shook his head. 'No doubt about it, this planet is blown wide open. We'll have to get you out fast. We'll have to get everyone out, but you first. Every ruff in Kurr will be looking for you, and you have no secondary identity to fall back on.'

'I don't even have a first identity.'

'True. You haven't had time to establish one. Paul is flying in, and he probably intends to fly right back out with you.'

The guard called from the stairway, 'We're about to have visitors. Joe is on his way up.'

'Right,' Rawner answered. 'Everything under control there? Come up and have a drink. It'd be silly to leave it for the ruffs.'

He filled a bowl for him and another for Joe, the fat tavern pourer, who entered from the wall panel. The pourer downed his in one gulp, wiped his lips, and remarked, 'You know, I liked this place.'

He went into the next room and returned a moment later, miraculously slender, wearing different clothing and carrying a wig.

'Need any money?' Rawner asked.

'I have plenty,' the pourer said, donning the wig. 'Del wants to know if any more props are needed. He's about to close shop.'

'No. There are plenty where we're going. Tell him to bring the sealant with him. He'll know what to do. Another drink, Supervisor?' He refilled Forzon's bowl and splashed the remainder into his own. 'Drink up, and we'll be on our way.'

They drained their bowls. Rawner got to his feet and

stood for a moment idly smacking a fist into an open hand. 'A lot of good work has gone up in this,' he said.

He opened the wall panel. The man named Del was already standing by with a spray gun. 'That sealant is good stuff,' Rawner said. 'In thirty seconds this panel will be a permanent part of the wall. I wouldn't use it if there was any chance that we'd need the place again.'

Joe, now an ex-pourer, led the way with a lighted taper. Forzon followed, other agents joined them from the next room and the floor below, and they moved in procession along the dark passageway to the upper floor of an adjoining house. For the next hour they followed a tortuous route that descended to tunnels and climbed to upper passageways, and twice they emerged to walk a short distance along one of Kurra's dark, narrow streets. Their destination was a tastefully furnished apartment in a concealed subcellar, and one man was waiting there at a table, gazing despondently into a half-filled drinking bowl. Paul Leblanc.

'Ready to go?' he asked Forzon.

Forzon seated himself wearily and shook his head when Leblanc pushed a drinking bowl toward him. He closed his eyes and slumped back in his chair. He had not relaxed since that fateful instant at the festival when Tor's music stopped. The long hours of tension had taken an inevitable toll. He was exhausted, but he was also nursing a seething resentment. Along the way it had suddenly occurred to him that he was the ranking officer on this planet, that whatever happened here was ultimately his responsibility, and that he had weakly surrendered his authority to subordinates and allowed them to shepherd him about with a saccharine solicitude better reserved for lost orphans.

'Is the supervising coordinator permitted to ask what is happening?' he murmured.

'The plane is waiting on the roof. There'll be plenty of time to talk later.'

Forzon jerked erect. 'We'll talk now,' he snapped. 'I have the feeling that we're playing right into Rastadt's hands.'

'Perhaps. But we have no choice. The planet is blown.'

'Who says so?'

'Rastadt—' Leblanc broke off, staring at Forzon.

'Have you seen him?'

Leblanc shook his head. 'The message was recorded while I was away: planet blown, make immediate arrangements to pull everyone out.'

'On a matter as momentous as this one, I'd think that the coordinator would deliver his orders in person and help to carry them out. Where is he?'

Leblanc did not answer.

'He blew the planet himself,' Forzon said. 'He did it deliberately, and he knows that we know that. Who arranged that warm Kurrian reception for me? Who tipped the king off to Team B's locations? Who furnished my ID photo for copying?'

'I agree,' Leblanc said tiredly. 'But we have no choice. If a planet is blown we have to pull out. It doesn't matter how, or by whom, or for what purpose. A basic principle of the Bureau's existence is at stake.'

'What does Rastadt stand to gain from it?'

'Nothing.'

'Think again. Here's a coordinator who's botched up his command and submitted false reports to Supreme Headquarters to keep himself out of trouble. Headquarters becomes suspicious and sends in a supervising coordinator. Rastadt easily bamboozles him, leads him into an ambush, and goes home thinking that his problem is solved. Suddenly he receives a message saying that the supervising coordinator has reached Team B safely. When did you send that message?'

'Just three days ago.'

Forzon nodded grimly. 'There you have it. Rastadt is no fool, and he knows that you people aren't fools. The only way he can save himself now is by eliminating everyone who knows about his treachery, and that means he has to to eliminate Team B. All of it, because by this time every

91

agent will have heard about my ambush. He's deliberately blown the planet in an attempt to destroy the evidence against him.'

Leblanc said thoughtfully, 'I was on my regular swing through the north. I filed an agenda. Probably I shouldn't have, but it's so routine that it's almost a reflex action. Rastadt knew I'd be out of touch with my headquarters for at least a week. So little was happening up there that I came back five days early – and found his message.' He turned. The others had gathered about the table and were listening intently. 'Since he knew that I wouldn't be there to receive the message, he only sent it to cover himself later on. He'll use it to prove that he was in close touch with the situation and gave us ample warning.'

'Every place the ruffs hit was known to those lackeys Rastadt wished onto us a few years back,' Sev Rawner said softly. 'Any place or identity they didn't know about is still secure.'

Leblanc nodded. 'Unfortunately, the planet is still blown. We'll have to pull out. I plan to take over base and place Rastadt and his staff under arrest pending formal hearings.'

'Are you willing to fight?' Rawner asked. 'They'll know that they face long prison terms. They may not give up easily.'

'We'll outnumber them four to one, and Team B could handle any base staff even if the odds were the other way around. The only problem is getting the team back there with our one plane. We'll work something out.'

'How many recording receivers does Team B operate?' Forzon asked.

'Just the one. Why?'

'Let's pretend we didn't receive Rastadt's message.'

'He'll repeat it whenever we contact base.'

'Then let's not contact base.'

'He'll have notified Supreme Headquarters. A ship is probably on its way now to evacuate us.'

'Then let's not show up to be evacuated.'

92

Leblanc gazed at him blankly. 'What *are* you driving at?'

'I'm saying that we have only Rastadt's word for it that the planet is blown, and Rastadt's word isn't worth much. Not to me, it isn't. What would happen if Team B cut all contact with base?'

'Rastadt would think we'd been wiped out.'

'Then let him think that.'

'IPR doesn't lose a complete field team without an investigation.'

'On a blown planet?'

'Supreme Headquarters would investigate,' Leblanc said slowly. 'It would assume that there must be survivors, and naturally it'd do everything it could to get them out. It'd go about it very cautiously, though.'

'What shape is Team B in right now?'

'Pressed. We'll be all right, though. All of us have alternate identities. We can hold out as long as necessary. It'll be an orderly withdrawal, not a rout.'

'We're not withdrawing,' Forzon announced. He looked up at a circle of confounded faces. Defensively he said again, 'We're not withdrawing.'

Leblanc protested, 'You're the supervising coordinator, but no officer has a right to contravene basic Bureau principles.'

'At what stage does a planet become blown?'

'When the natives—'

'How many natives know that Team B is operating in Kurr?'

No one answered.

'There's no doubt that Rastadt is in league with the king,' Forzon said. 'Treason seems like an incredible length to go merely to keep a job as coordinator, but there isn't time now to unravel his motives. The king knows we're here, but how many other natives know it? Has the king posted a proclamation that Kurr is invaded from outer space?'

'I don't think he'd want his subjects to know it,' Leblanc conceded.

'Right. The planet is not blown, and I doubt that Rastadt will be in a hurry to tell Supreme Headquarters that it is. Since his object is to eliminate Team B, he won't want an investigation until he's certain that he's been successful. In the meantime – well, we have time.'

'Time for what?'

'Time to accomplish Team B's mission.'

'To accomplish—' Leblanc stared at him. 'Ah!' he exclaimed, suddenly radiant. 'You have a plan. Excellent!'

'Well, I—'

Leblanc leaped to his feet. 'Close every station Rastadt's men knew, and see that every agent they knew switches identities. Rastadt may be listening, so I want no radio communication until further notice. We can use the plane to scatter couriers through the outlying districts, and they'll be days ahead of the king's ruffs.'

'Rastadt's men knew about this place,' Rawner said.

'We're moving out now. I'll be at Ann's with the supervisor. You send out the couriers, Sev, and then report to me there.' He seized Forzon's hand and shook it gleefully. 'That's what I call *positive* thinking. Make Supreme Headquarters a present of a democracy in Kurr, and there won't be enough interest in whether the planet was blown or not to require a formal hearing.'

At dawn they were seated around a table in Ann Cory's residence, a small apartment with a single window high above the city's wall. Leblanc was there, and Sev Rawner, whose blindly-staring eyes still made Forzon blink uncomfortably, and Karl Trom, a burly man with a pungent aroma of sawdust who wore arm-length leather gloves and a jacket that hung low in the front like an apron.

Ann Cory, still in the guise of a venerable hag, tripped lightly into the room, looked about in surprise, and called to Forzon, 'You didn't know me!'

94

'It was the bad light,' Forzon said. 'In the daytime I'd know that turned up nose no matter how many wrinkles you put around it.'

It could have been his imagination that she blushed. She stepped behind a screen, and a few minutes later emerged as a robust, red-faced matron.

'What it amounts to,' Leblanc said, disappointment throbbing in every word, 'is that you don't actually have a plan.'

'That's what it amounts to,' Forzon admitted.

'I suppose I was expecting too much. You've hardly been here long enough to find out what the problem is, but I thought perhaps an entirely different viewpoint—'

Forzon pushed back his chair and went to the window. A magnificent sunrise had begun to arrange itself before his startled eyes, and he watched for some moments, completely enraptured, before he became aware of the uncomfortable silence in the room behind him. The others were regarding him with puzzlement.

He stepped aside with a magnanimous gesture. 'I'll be glad to share it with you.'

'Share what?' Leblanc demanded.

'The sunrise.'

They stirred doubtfully.

'Come and look,' Forzon said.

'I really don't see—'

'*Look!*'

Each took a turn at the window, shrugged, returned to his seat. Ann remained the longest, alternately peering at the sunrise and directing searching sideglances at Forzon.

Finally she turned away, and Forzon said sharply, 'That won't do. You looked, but none of you admired it.'

'Does this have something to do with the plan that you don't have yet?' Leblanc asked.

'It has something to do with the reason none of Team B's plans have worked. Team B doesn't understand the

95

people of Kurr. It won't until its agents take the time, now and then, to admire a sunrise.'

'I suppose I should ask you to explain that, but we really have more critical things to do than play with riddles.'

'I'll explain anyway,' Forzon said. 'From where I'm standing I can see a full company of guards drawn up on the wall – looking at the sunrise. Every window that's visible from here has faces in it – looking at the sunrise. When the natives are that intently concerned with something, it behooves Team B to take notice of it. How many agents were at the king's festival last night?'

'We always have several in attendance.'

'As reporters, to let you know if any untoward events occur,' Forzon said caustically. 'How many attend because they enjoy festivals?'

'Observation is an important part of our job,' Leblanc protested. 'Last night we knew what happened to Tor within minutes after the festival was over. It was the first time in anyone's recollection that a king of Kurr committed an unwise act in public, and it meant that King Rovva was in a rarely foul mood, even for him. Sev had a hunch and posted an alert immediately, which was why we didn't lose anyone.'

'Have you heard why the king committed an unwise act?' Ann asked.

Leblanc looked at her inquiringly.

'Night before last a plane flew here from Larnor. Wace got a beam on it, entirely by accident. We just got word.'

'Flew *here*? To Kurra?'

'It landed near here. Probably in the royal preserves.'

'Rastadt,' Leblanc muttered. 'Coming to turn the king loose on Team B.'

'The king was en route back from his seaside castle,' Ann said. 'He didn't reach Kurra until late yesterday afternoon. That was the reason for the festival – to celebrate his homecoming. Shortly after he arrived the ruffs began making inquiries with the supervisor's portrait, and late that evening the king was still angry enough to lose his head in public and send Kurr's greatest *torril* player to a one-hand village. I'm sorry, Supervisor.' She smiled sweetly. 'You were saying that Team B doesn't understand the people of Kurr?'

Feeling utterly ridiculous, Forzon did not reply.

'And you do,' Ann went on, still smiling sweetly. 'I'll be interested to see this plan of yours. How long will it take you to work it out?'

'I haven't any idea.'

'The immediate question is *where* he will work it out,' Leblanc said. 'This is no time to be establishing an identity, not with the king's ruffs on the prowl. We could keep him in a safe place, but that would amount to locking him in a closet. He wouldn't be able to look out of a window very often, no matter how much he admires sunrises. Not in Kurra, and I suspect that he'd be even less safe in the country. Strangers are much more conspicuous there. Except – Cultural Survey. Can you paint, Supervisor? An artist can go anywhere, no questions asked.'

'I can paint,' Forzon said, 'but my technique wouldn't be up to these artists, and it'd take some practice before I could use that paint. My first efforts would probably be a mess.'

'Your first efforts would have to be adequate. What else is there? Could you play a *torril*?'

'On the level of one of those children at the musicians' village – but only if I had some time to practice and it was a young child.'

'It looks as if you'll have to stay in Kurra,' Leblanc said resignedly. 'I don't like that. If they run house-to-house searches you'll be constantly on the move, and no matter how careful we are there's always the chance of a slipup.'

'Will we need to be in touch with him regularly?' Ann asked.

'No. Not if he's in a safe place. But it'd have to be a situation where his doing nothing won't attract attention to him – since he can't do anything.' Forzon winced. 'Besides,' Leblanc went on, 'he'll need plenty of leisure to work out this plan of his.'

'I know just the place,' Ann said. 'We'll send him to a one-hand village.'

'Very funny,' Forzon drawled. 'And if they're full up, King Rovva probably has an unused guest room at the castle.'

But Leblanc was nodding his head thoughtfully. 'The very thing. There wouldn't be a safer place in Kurr. They might make him work, though, and what could he do?'

'Give him a trade that the village couldn't use.'

Leblanc snapped his fingers. 'Valet. There can't be much call for a valet in a one-hand village, and the uniform coat has sleeves. Also, the royal servants have their heads shaved, which would be all the disguise he'd need. He was a valet in the royal service and he – let's see – spilled a platter of *sullux*. Everyone knows that *sullux* is the king's favourite dish, and spilling it would guarantee an instantaneous initiation into the one-hand clan. If the village insists on his working, he'll have an excuse for learning a new trade. He should know something about valeting, though. Who could give him some quick lessons?'

'Clyde?' Ann suggested.

'Get him here. If this had happened – let's see – last night right after the festival, he'd be able to travel late today. We'll send him out through the south gate, and the guards will turn their backs on him. A one-hand village will be the ideal environment for working out his plan. It's practically Kurr in microcosm. Kurr with time standing still. There'll be people from all walks of life, including a large number who have had one too many personal contacts with King Rovva. The supervisor can learn from them, and as he gets ideas he can try them out himself.'

'Don't forget the uniform,' Ann said.

'To be sure. The coat will have to be oversize. He'll wear his left arm inside the coat, and we'll strap a phony half-arm to his shoulder. Supervisor, you'd better start right now learning to do everything with your right hand.'

NINE

Affecting the dejected, uncertain stride of the banished, Forzon moved haltingly through the shadowed streets. He experienced no difficulty in adopting the proper mien; he *felt* dejected and uncertain. Pedestrians turned their backs on him, carts halted until he passed, even the children scurried for cover, though the boldest lingered in doorways to peer out at him.

Ann Cory, again a venerable hag, limped ahead of him to show him the way. Now and again he caught a glimpse of a familiar profile: Sev Rawner tottering across a side-street; Joe Sornel, formerly a fat tavern pourer but now a slender tradesman, standing in the door of his shop; Hance Ultman sitting with downcast eyes in a halted cart. Every available agent had been mobilized to see him safely from the city, but he raised his eyes from the worn paving stones only to follow Ann's turnings, and he saw few of them.

At the city gate one guard stepped toward him, noticed the empty, flopping sleeve, and scornfully turned on his heel. Forzon moved on through the gate and plodded along the dusty road that led south.

Methodically he placed one foot before the other and kept his eyes on the rippling dust. He met no one. Traffic veered off the road and waited for him to pass. Those who overtook him turned to the fields to go around and did not look back.

Under the caressing warmth of the late afternoon sun his scarlet uniform became damp with perspiration and acquired a dulling veneer of dust. The forced inertness of

99

his left arm tantalized him. His shaven head itched fiercely. Mild as these distractions were, he cursed them because they impaired his ability to concentrate.

He had much that he needed to think about.

The one-hand villages were tiny, isolated societies, so effectively detached from Kurrian life that Team B had never found a use for them, had never investigated them systematically. Although the IPR agents methodically compiled such information as came their way, the blunt fact was that they knew next to nothing about life in a one-hand village. Team B would keep an eye on Forzon until he reached his destination, but once there he would be on his own, in an utterly strange society – with a price on his head.

Much to his own surprise he found that this did not worry him. His gnawing anxiety resulted from his stupidity in allowing himself to be manipulated into a commitment to solve the problem of Kurr. Admittedly this was his assignment, but he had managed to ignore it on the reasonable assumption that a Cultural Survey officer's responsibilities should be restricted to matters concerning culture. The IPR Bureau thought otherwise; after four centuries of highly competent bungling it was ready to grasp irrationally at any straw, and at the moment that straw was CS Sector Supervisor Jef Forzon.

Kurr had to be converted into a democracy without apparent outside interference, and quickly, before Rastadt's machinations took effect and Supreme Headquarters stepped in to force the withdrawal of Team B. The job was Forzon's. He had accepted it, had committed himself.

'Get your plans ready,' Leblanc said to him in parting. 'As soon as we're reorganized, we'll go to work on them.'

The only thing Forzon knew well was culture, and how the devil could anyone be incited to revolt over culture? Painting? The governor who placed a tax on painting had been promptly dispatched to a one-hand village. Music? Obviously the Kurrians were an intensely musical people.

They loved music passionately, they sang beautifully, they produced masterful performers, but – revolution?

Kurrian poetry seemed stylized and degenerate, perhaps the inevitable result of an hereditary system by which only the son of a poet could become a poet; but under the same rigid system the painters maintained a fresh and vigorous craftsmanship and the musicians had attained magnificent heights of creative expression and virtuosity. The only poems he had heard were vapid paeans to the beauty of nature or the nobility and wisdom of the king. Could he persuade a poet to construct satiric verses in praise of the king's evil? Probably not, and the instantaneous banishment to a one-hand village of the first poet who did so would be unlikely to encourage imitators.

'All I have to do,' he thought wryly, 'is to communicate the need for revolution in some popular form of expression that the people will embrace spontaneously. The formal arts are out of it. Their practitioners are trapped in the rigidity of closed orders and inherited traditions, besides which they are too vulnerable. Either the expression has to be so diffused that no individual can be held responsible and punished, or the individuals apparently responsible have to be in a position of impunity. There isn't any and there aren't any.'

Songs might be the answer. One song that became really popular could do more damage than a dozen unfair taxes, but he had no idea how to go about obtaining songs that would be sufficiently appealing. No Kurrian would dare to write them, and Forzon doubted that he could do it himself. They would require a sure feeling for the Kurrian musical and poetic idioms and an astute understanding of the people. He had neither.

Fretfully he prodded his imagination. A caricature of the king hacking off a man's arm? It would have to be superbly done if it were to compete with the quality of art available to everyone, and to obtain enough prints for an effective distribution they would have to be mass produced. The Rule of One. Damn!

A sudden awareness of danger brought Forzon to a halt. A cart was approaching him from the rear; unlike the others, it had not turned off the road to go around him.

He did not dare to look back. He started off again, quickening his pace, lengthening his stride, and the cart's creaking crescendoed steadily as it gradually overtook him. The ugly *esg* came abreast of him and eyed him with wary snorts as it slowly pulled ahead. Forzon stepped aside, and at that moment the cart stopped.

He turned slowly. It was a typical Kurrian cart, with two wheels and a box formed of pegged boards. The driver sat at the front on a slab laid across the box, the guide rope clutched in his right hand, his eyes fixed staringly on the road ahead.

In the cart lay a single object, richly carved and polished, inlaid with gold. A *torril*. Forzon looked dumbly from *torril* to driver and then to the driver's empty left sleeve that flapped pathetically in the stirring breeze.

Helping himself awkwardly with his right hand, Forzon climbed into the cart. Tor, great musician the previous evening and now a miserable outcast, flicked the guide rope. The *esg* moved forward.

For three nights and days they were on the road. At night they took turns leading the *esg* with a lighted torch, one of them walking ahead while the other dozed, until the exhausted animal refused to go further and went to sleep in its traces. Forzon did more than his share of the walking and most of the driving. Tor spent his waking hours racked with pain. He made no complaint, but his shockingly pale face, constricted limbs and clenched teeth bespoke indescribable agonies, and in his feverish sleep he moaned and whimpered constantly.

Food and drink were given to them when they wanted it. They had only to halt by a farmhouse or in a village street.

Presently a basket and a crock would be thrust into the cart and the bearer would hurry away. Through the long, exhausting journey no one spoke to them and they spoke to no one, not even to each other.

On the afternoon of the fourth day they approached one of the king's garrisons. These tall stone buildings, looking starkly out of place in their rural surroundings, were located along the main roads a day's journey apart. Invariably the sentry had turned his back as they passed, but this one, when he noticed their empty sleeves, stepped into the road and pointed. They turned from the dusty main road and followed faint ruts that wound back into the hills.

At dusk they looked down on a picture book village, nestled peacefully in a deep valley. Animals grazed on the surrounding hills, orchards dotted the landscape, and the level valley floor was blocked into gardens and grainfields. The buildings, unlike those of other rural villages, were built of cut stone, the smooth white surfaces dazzling even in the shadowed valley. Flowers lined the streets and walks. The scene was charming, and Forzon regarded it with horror.

The village was so *large*.

Only later did he remember that this village was but one of many.

Across the valley a row of buildings stood far up on the hillside, overlooking the village. Another solitary building loomed just ahead of them where the rutted track dipped down into the valley. Tor halted the cart beside it, and they waited until the *esg* began to stomp and wheeze impatiently.

Finally a man appeared, and while they sat with eyes averted he scrutinized them, muttered disgustedly, 'A musician and a valet,' and motioned them on. Only when he had turned away did Forzon dare to look at him directly. His sidelong impression had been correct: this man was not one-handed.

As they approached the village an elderly man came hobbling to meet them, a one-handed man, and he greeted

103

them with a silent nod and guided them through the village streets. On the far side of the village they halted beside a new building; beyond it another was being built. The village was growing.

They climbed from the cart. The building was typically Kurrian but with a long row of doors facing onto the street, and their guide opened one of these and pointed. Forzon entered a small room furnished with straw-stuffed pallet, a chair, a table with a set of hand carved eating and drinking bowls.

For the first time the old man spoke. 'Does your arm need attention? We have a doctor.'

'It does not need attention,' Forzon said.

'You are fortunate. Usually an arm does not heal so quickly.'

Forzon agreed that he was fortunate.

The village's governors, the old man said, desired to pay their respects whenever Forzon felt able to receive them. Forzon gravely considered this and announced that he would receive them whenever they wished to call. The old man thanked him and went next door to talk with Tor, and a short time later a committee of village elders came to extend the village's official welcome.

They confessed apologetically that a valet, even the king's valet, had no occupational standing in a one-hand village. There were jobs of various kinds that were open to anyone. Men were needed to carry materials to the masons at work on the new buildings. Those cultivating the fields or looking after the flocks always welcomed assistance. There were artisans who might consider taking him as an apprentice, and sometimes artists accepted helpers for menial tasks, though they were restrained by oath from disclosing the secrets of their skills to outsiders. If Forzon chose he could work at any form of employment open to him. If he preferred he could do nothing at all. No one would interfere with him, and the one law of the village was that he must interfere with no one.

The Great King, in his noble generosity, provided anything that the village lacked. The surpluses from fields and flocks, and all that the artisans produced that the village did not need, were sold by the king, and some of the money credited to the village to buy luxuries for all. It was, the governors assured Forzon, speaking slowly as if to convince themselves, a good life. And while Forzon could remain idle if he chose, they thought he would be happier if he worked.

Forzon thanked them for their advice. In the next room the doctor was visiting Tor, and they seemed as eager to escape the tortured cries and sobs as Forzon was to have them leave. They quickly described the order of life in the village and departed.

Following their instructions, Forzon went first to obtain an issue of clothing. He examined this with some trepidation, but the upper garments fitted loosely enough to conceal his arm, so his disguise remained secure. The clothing proved that while the Great King might be generous, he certainly was not profligate with his royal cloth: every left sleeve was half-length.

At the community kitchen in the center of the village a one-handed woman silently filled Forzon's eating and drinking bowls. He carried them back to his quarters and ate slowly, meditating on the wisdom of Team B in sending him to this place.

The law of non-interference augured well for his safety, and the right to leisure guaranteed him the time he needed to work out his plans for Kurr. The critical question seemed to be whether he could, in this village of the living dead, produce plans that would have any validity among the living.

The buildings that stood high on the hillside were dormitories, and from these there came at dawn a slender procession of one-handed women to work in the kitchen. Twice daily they set forth food, and the men carried it to their

105

quarters to eat. There seemed to be no social contacts between men and women and few between men. Artisans worked in pairs if a task required two hands, but their conversation was limited to a word of instruction, a muttered question, an answering glance. It was a village of tense silences.

It was a congregation of the nameless. Names belonged to the past, and the inmates' pasts were kept locked within them.

Forzon's resolution to get to work immediately had a brief but unequal struggle with his natural curiosity about his surroundings and lost. For several days he wandered from workshop to workshop, silently watching the silent workers. Skilled metalsmiths shaped beautifully engraved objects of gleaming copper and silver for the king's trade. Weavers, two of them working at a loom, turned out handsome rugs and cloth, each pattern a superb individual creation. Others, performing with unbelievable coordination, turned piles of straw into strikingly designed baskets and mats. There were wood carvers and cobblers and potters and carpenters and masons.

Only the work of the artists disappointed, and for a long time that perplexed Forzon. He finally deduced that Kurrian art was an art of pictorial realism, of familiar settings and people, and in the environment of a one-hand village there was no place for it. Pictorial reminders of the bleak life that they led would have been repugnant to the inmates. They lived with their memories, and no artist could reproduce another man's memories. Of all the dwellings in Kurr, only the whitewashed walls of the one-hand villages were barren of art.

Nor would the artists have cared to depict the village and its one-handed residents. They painted exclusively from their own pasts. Not people – those memories were too intensely personal to bring to visual reality – but places. One elderly artist had filled the walls of his workroom with painting after painting of the same small, flower-adorned cottage. Here it stood in the gleaming light of full summer, its exterior freshly painted, its flowers a riot of color. Here it received the onslaught of an unseasonal summer storm. Here it stood under a mellow harvest sun, with baskets of fruit piled by the door; here in winter, stripped bare of its foliage by a chill wind; here in spring, with the first green harbingers of the coming season. The cottage aged, acquired a fresh coat of paint, and again endured the full cycle of storms and seasons, each painstakingly and masterfully depicted, that slowly weathered it to old age and eventual rejuvenation.

There was no outside market for such work. Citizens who could easily obtain paintings of their own living present had no interest in mementos of another man's dead past.

As an art critic Forzon found the paintings disappointing; as a human being their tragic poignancy moved him to tears.

Among all of these men of varied talents and occupations Forzon was most interested in his neighbor Tor, who like Forzon was doing nothing.

The *torril* stood in the center of his tiny room. Tor sat nearby on a wood stool, misery etched indelibly on his good looking young face. Several times Forzon heard – or thought he heard – the pleasant twang of a plucked string. But he could not be certain.

An artist, assuming that he was right handed, could paint without loss of skill with his left arm removed. A singer could sing, a poet put words together. A one-handed artisan could manage very good work. Tor's had to be the ultimate tragedy.

It should have been possible to play a *torril* after a fashion with one hand, to pick out music of simple structure and limited range, but obviously to a musician of Tor's consummate virtuosity this would be infinitely worse than no music at all.

When Forzon noticed that Tor was not eating regularly, he broke the village's basic law and interfered. He began

107

to stop by for Tor's bowl when he went to the kitchen. Tor accepted the food with a nod of thanks, though he ate little. They spoke for the first time when Forzon, on an impulse, asked for music lessons. 'Could you teach me to play?' he said.

Interest flashed in Tor's face and quickly faded. 'No,' he answered curtly.

'I could sit opposite you,' Forzon said. 'Your hand on one side and mine on the other. We could play together.'

'It would be impossible.'

Even in a village of the living dead, Tor remained faithful to his musician's oath.

A young wood carver was fashioning a large drinking bowl, and around the inside rim he carved clusters of *kwim* berries, a fruit from which one of the light sweet Kurrian wines was made. Each day one more berry was separated from the smooth wood surface, its oblong shape meticullously cut in relief with surgical precision, its beady surface shaped with loving care. One day, one berry. A leaf, with its delicate network of veins and its crinkly edges, probably took much longer. There were ten to fifteen berries in a cluster, and when he finished there would be at least ten fully leafed clusters around the bowl's interior. Perhaps he would also carve the bottom and the outer surface. Forzon calculated that the bowl might occupy the carver for two years or more, and went his way shaking his head.

Thus time was measured in a one-hand village. One berry a day, carved in relief on a drinking bowl. Or, in a painting, one flower on the facade of a dwelling, brought to life with almost microscopic strokes of a brush, each petal quivering with dew. One brief line of poetry, for which a thousand words were measured for meaning and weighed accent by accent and rejected.

Most of the artisans and common workers performed with smooth, mechanical efficiency, but their tasks were shaped by mundane necessities. The villagers had to be fed and clothed and housed so that the artistic among them could relieve their tormented souls in inconsequential perfections at the rate of one berry a day, and the utterly lost could spend their waking hours staring at something beyond infinity.

Once he had satisfied his initial curiosity about the village Forzon became one of the starers, but he strained, not at infinity, but at Kurr and its people. Day after day he attempted to envision this population of (outside the one-hand villages) happy, prosperous people in the throes of revolution, and he could not. The ideas he devised seemed no more potent than pin pricks, and a pin prick, even when it drew blood, rarely had fatal consequences.

He weighed his ideas one by one and discarded them and in the end nothing remained but a resurrection of his speculation about popular subversive songs. Fate had placed Forzon in contact with the one great musician in Kurr who had a festering grievance against the king, but Tor's prevailing mood of stark tragedy did not augur well for the lightly satiric touch that such a song would need. Could Tor create this kind of music? It seemed worth a try.

There remained the problem of words, and Forzon failed utterly in his attempts to maneuver the poets away from their lyrical fancies of half forgotten sunsets and their rhymed involvements in the tragedies of fading flowers. If words were to be written, he would have to do it himself.

After a prolonged struggle he produced a single stanza:

> *A man of trust*
> *Inhaled some dust*
>   *And sneezed.*
> *He meant no harm,*
> *But – 'Off with his arm!'*
>   *King Rovva wheezed.*

He carefully lettered the lines on a scrap of parchment and took them to Tor. 'Have you ever created music for a song?' he asked.

Tor wrenched his gaze from some personal bottomless void and regarded Forzon sullenly, his eyes uncomprehending.

'I have some lines I would like to have sung,' Forzon said. 'Could you create the music?'

Tor reached out with his right hand and took the parchment. As Forzon watched anxiously the musician slowly scanned the lines. Suddenly his head jerked back, and he stared at Forzon with wide-eyed astonishment. 'Treason!' he blurted.

Forzon recovered the parchment and hastily returned to his quarters, where he burned it and pulverized the ashes.

'So much for my pin prick,' he thought bitterly. 'And how is it possible to plan revolt in a land where even the victims of a king's hideous cruelty blanch in horror at a whisper of treason?'

In the darkness he would leave his room and stumble about the rolling countryside, squinting at the diminutive moon and searching vainly for an inspiration, an idea, a fact, anything at all that he could convert into a semblance of a plan for Team B to act upon. Each passing day saw another berry take shape on the carver's drinking bowl and, Forzon fancied, turned a few of the subterraneous hairs on his shaven head to gray. At any moment he might receive word that Team B had completed its reorganization.

He had no plan, and inspiration proved as elusive as the small Kurrian moon.

TEN

They came singly and in pairs, most of them walking, their faces dazed, exhausted, taut with pain.

Newcomers. When the last room of one dormitory was occupied a new building stood ready and foundation stones had been laid for the next. One ghastly day there came a

110

group of ten. The village elders received them imperturbably and rushed work on the next building.

Forzon had been in the village for a Kurrian month, thirty-seven days, before he witnessed the arrival of a woman. An elder received her with the usual silent compassion and guided her cart toward the women's dormitories on the hillside, and as they passed Forzon he noted that she was middle-aged, that her face was ravaged with weeping, and finally that she possessed a turned up nose of a configuration he had sworn never to forget.

Ann Cory, B627, slyly gave him a sidelong glance and a wink. Forzon followed at a distance and watched the elder assign her to her quarters.

He met her after dark, and they walked together in the dim moonlight to the top of a hill and sat looking down on the deeply shadowed village. Tapers burned in the home of the king's agent, the crafty-faced two-handed individual who had greeted Tor and Forzon with such disgust; but his home at the far end of the valley was remote from the village and faced away from it, and so did the agent except on reckoning day, when he supervised the loading of the village's surpluses for market. Lights were rarely seen in the village, and when they did burn late they invariably signified sickness or death.

'It's a gloomy place,' Ann observed.

'It's a horrible place,' Forzon said.

'At least you'll have the satisfaction of putting an end to such places.'

Disconcerted, Forzon sought to change the subject. 'How are things outside?' he asked lamely.

'Confused. Rastadt knew more than we thought, curse him, and we had several near catastrophes, but we scraped through. Paul is putting the pieces back together. We'll soon be ready for action in Kurra, but it will take longer to get established again in the rural districts. The king has his ruffs chasing everywhere, and any stranger is instantly suspect – except in a one-hand village.'

'Have you had any direct word from Rastadt?'

'No. We cut off all communication, as you suggested. He'll know that we've gone underground, and he'll know that the king hasn't caught a single agent – if the king is willing to admit it. Even if he does Rastadt may not believe him, and since the coordinator's advice has put the whole country in a turmoil without producing any discernible result, the king may have stopped believing Rastadt. It's a beautiful situation, and the two of them deserve each other. What do you have for us to work on?'

'Not much,' Forzon admitted. He told her of his idea about the songs, and of Tor's reaction.

She pronounced a firm verdict. 'It wouldn't have worked anyway. That sort of thing comes out spontaneously when the people are ready for it. Even if you got a song written, anyone hearing it would howl for a king's officer. First we must make revolution a necessity. Once we achieve that, the people won't be shocked at the thought of treason.'

'I see,' Forzon said glumly. 'The Bureau's ninth law, I suppose.'

Looking at her dim profile, he thought nostalgically of the lovely young girl she had been at base.

She seemed to sense his disapproving scrutiny. 'It's a terrible disguise,' she said. 'It makes my shoulders too broad, and I have to keep fighting an impulse to punch someone with my left hand. I barely escaped having my head shaved. At the last minute Sven turned up the information that a castle charwoman doesn't, she just has it cut short, so I got off with wearing a wig. It's uncomfortable and I can't get into any hair-pulling contests, but at least when I leave here I won't have to go into hiding until my hair grows out. Anyway, here I am.'

He kissed her – kissed a memory, really, of a girl with golden hair and a rustling gown and strangely exotic scent; but this was Ann Cory, Gurnil B627, an IPR Bureau agent on an assignment. Her soft lips yielded to his momentarily, and then she jerked away. 'I'm supposed to go over your plans with you and tell you what's possible and what isn't,' she said brusquely. 'What do you have.'

'Well – I've been wondering about Tor,' he faltered.

'What about him?'

'He was the greatest *torril* player in Kurr – sort of a national hero, someone said.'

'Yes. He was.'

'And the king's having his arm removed at a public festival was the most stupid move a king has made since Team B first checked in here.'

'Mmm – perhaps. I won't speak for all four hundred years of Team B history, but it certainly represented an unusual level of stupidity for King Rovva.'

'Wouldn't there be some way to make Tor the symbol of everything that's bad about the king's regime?'

'It's too late. A musician can be a national hero when he's playing, but when he stops he's quickly forgotten. There are other *torril* players who are almost as good as Tor was, and a few of them might become even better. The day after it happened there would have been a remote chance of arousing the people if Tor had been willing to cooperate, which I doubt. Now there's another Tor.'

'I see. What we have here,' Forzon said thoughtfully, 'is a people who are so passionately aesthetic that they are blind to moral ugliness. The king's acts are ugly. His form of government and his exercise of it are ugly, but artistic beauty flourishes, and that's what the people want.'

'It's a little deep for me, but I guess so.'

'Has Team B ever speculated as to why the king operates these one-hand villages?'

'The villages are older than Team B. King Rovva is simply carrying on a tradition, though with a vengeance. The villages' populations have increased enormously during his reign.'

'The mere fact that he maintains them so generously suggests that he's vulnerable,' Forzon mused. 'What the villages do, actually, is provide a place of concealment for the victims of the king's ugliness.'

'True enough. Is that what the plan is about? To get the ugliness into the open?'

'I doubt that the people would see it. They have a mental block. Actually, it's always been in the open for anyone who cared to take note of it. If the citizens thought at all about the number of one-handed victims traveling to the villages they'd have to arrive at a significant conclusion. But they turn their backs. On the other hand, they're willing to defy the king if he interferes with their love of beauty.'

'How do you figure that?'

'From the conduct of the woman who hid me when I arrived in Kurr. I gave her the priest's robe, and because it was beautiful she was willing to defy the king's law to keep it, even at the risk of her life. As a working hypothesis – when the king's ugliness interferes with a citizen's love of beauty, the citizen will defy the king.'

'What do you want us to do? Place an order for a million robes?'

Forzon did not answer.

'I'm afraid that I missed the point,' she said.

'I may have missed it myself. I just realized that I do have an idea, but I don't know what to do with it. Is there a musical instrument in Kurr that can be played with one hand?'

'I can't think of any. What do you want it for?'

'For Tor. The man is a musical genius, and the loss of music is killing him. I'd like to find something he could play.'

'I don't think there is anything. Not on the art level, anyway. What angle are you working on?'

'No angle. For the moment I'd just like to give Tor an instrument to play. What happened next would depend on what he did with it.'

114

'Is that what's been occupying your time?' she demanded. 'An instrument for Tor?'

The vehemence of her question startled him. 'Not exactly,' he answered. 'But I would like to find out—'

'You'd like to know if he's adaptable enough to learn another instrument?'

'I'd have to know that before I could—'

'Do you consider Team B's mission as unimportant as all that? Men and women have been risking their lives daily just to be ready to carry out your plans. Paul has been working furiously to establish a new system of communication so we'll be able to move quickly the moment you're ready. Team B deserves better of you than this – this moping over the morale of an ex-musician. It's a noble, humanitarian concern, I suppose, but what is Tor to Team B?' She got to her feet abruptly, walked a short distance down the slope, and stood with her back to him looking out across the dark valley.

He answered calmly, 'Everything – I think.'

'I'm sorry,' she said. 'Your training has been different from ours. Naturally you'd look at things differently. We should have realized – the Bureau should have realized – but you seemed like such an alert, resourceful person, and from the way you talked we naturally assumed—'

'Ann!' Forzon exclaimed. 'I'm going to invoke the Rule of One!'

She spun around to face him. Her features were indistinct in the feeble glow of Kurr's miniature moon, but there was no mistaking the incredulity in her voice. 'You can't! Not just like that. You have to submit the suggestion to Supreme Headquarters and explain just what you want to do and why it's necessary to your plan and why the job can't be done some other way and what the probable technological impact might be. Supreme Headquarters will study the request very carefully and perhaps ask for several dozen supplemental reports, and then it'll file it away for a few years. By the time it gets around to rejecting your request you'll have thought of a better approach that doesn't need it. No one has *ever* used the Rule of One!'

'I'm cut off from Supreme Headquarters,' Forzon said. 'I can't submit my idea for approval, but – since I'm in charge here – I certainly have an obligation to take emergency action when I deem it necessary, and right now the most necessary thing on this planet is to find an instrument for Tor. I'm going to give him a trumpet.'

She took a step toward him. 'You fool! Haven't you at least a vague notion of the number of technological innovations a trumpet would require? Rule of One, indeed!'

'A primitive trumpet,' Forzon said patiently. 'A trumpet without valves. At some stage in their musical development most worlds evolve a variant of it, and it can be a splendid art instrument. All that's required to make one is a metal tube bent into the proper shape. If the Kurrian metal workers know how to make a tube I wouldn't be giving them any innovation, just a new use for what they already have.' He paused, and then went on meditatively, 'Except perhaps for the mouthpiece. It's the mouthpiece that converts a crude noisemaker into an art instrument – it has to have a special flat-cupped design to be really effective. It does seem strange that the Kurrians have no wind instruments. Still – the trumpet evolves from the horn, and the earliest horns are usually animal horns. All of the animals I've seen on this world have been hornless. Some primitive peoples have a shell trumpet, though. Is there an animal life on Gurnil with a shell that could be adapted to musical use?'

'Goodbye,' she said.

'There's no need to hurry back. No one makes a bed check in a one-hand village. If we want to wander about at night that's our own business. This rule of non-interference is very useful.'

'I'm leaving. I only came here to see you – to get those great plans of yours. I'll tell Paul that you're too busy ministering to a depressed musician to be bothered. If I walk fast I can reach the nearest Team B station before dawn, and we of the IPR Bureau have work to do. So – goodbye.'

'Wait!' Forzon pleaded. 'This business about Tor—'

'Is very interesting, I'm sure. You'll have plenty of time for it, because I'm afraid it'll be a long time before we can furnish you with a secure identity. In the meantime you'll be perfectly safe here.'

She moved off into the night, and he stood looking after her for a long time. Finally he returned to his quarters. For the remainder of the night he sat cross-legged on his pallet, lost in thought, and as soon as it was light enough to work he went rummaging in the waste bins for scraps of parchment. He spent most of the morning scratching designs on them.

When he had one that satisfied him he took it to the metal-smiths: a drawing of a valveless trumpet.

ELEVEN

They gathered around him and studied the drawing perplexedly. In the background bellows hissed, crucibles poured out heat and smoke, and metal clanged incessantly on metal. Forzon shouted a suggestion that they go outside where they could talk.

'Musical – instrument?' one of them echoed doubtfully, when Forzon finished his explanation.

The tube they understood. Yes – narrow at this end and gradually becoming larger. And of a certain size. All of that they understood.

But – musical instrument? Where were the strings?

They readily agreed to undertake the project. The design was interesting, especially the tapering tube and the odd

117

loop in the center, and that was reason enough for fashioning one of the strange things. When they finished he could use it for anything he liked. For all they cared he could even make music with it, though they didn't understand how that was to be done.

They set about making a trumpet.

Three days later Forzon inspected the result and was appalled.

The simple symmetry of the single loop in Forzon's sketch had seemed a reflection on their skill; they substituted a complicated coil that made Forzon fearful that violence had been done to his careful mathematical calculations on the length and taper of the instrument's bore. Not comprehending the acoustical function of the flaring bell, they executed it with the full force of their artistic ingenuity, producing an undulating, funnel-like arrangement that opened onto a massive, magnificently polished disc. Their mouthpiece was a perfectly-formed cup without an air passage.

Forzon requested several design changes, which they immediately proceeded to modify beyond recognition, and the finished instrument bore no more than a remote resemblance to his concept of a trumpet.

He thought that it might do. After they had ornamented it from bell to mouthpiece with exquisite engravings, they reluctantly surrendered it to him and trailed along curiously as he carried it to Tor's quarters.

Tor, resentful of this unwelcome visitation, at first stubbornly refused to touch the instrument. When finally he accepted it he held it awkwardly, puzzled for a few moments over its possible uses, and returned it to Forzon with a shrug. Forzon raised it to his lips and blew.

The tone was curiously mellow – whether because of its peculiar shape or because of the unscientifically designed mouthpiece Forzon could not decide – but the instrument blew with startling ease. Forzon, a rank musical amateur, had no difficulty in producing a series of tones that sounded not remotely unlike music.

Tor listened wonderingly. He took the trumpet again, made fumbling efforts to blow, and eventually produced a tone. Delight touched his face. He blew again and again. Face screwed up and flushed, panting for breath between efforts, he forced out a series of high notes, floundered until he discovered their lower octaves, and began to search for a scale. Forzon quietly withdrew.

In the street outside, one of the metalsmiths scratched his head and regarded Forzon with open admiration. 'You know,' he said, 'I'd like one of those things for myself.'

For the next few days Tor's struggle to master the trumpet drove Forzon into long walks to escape the abrupt, smearing blasts of sound, occasioned murmuring throughout the village, and finally brought the governors to Tor's door to investigate. The sacred rule of non-interference seemed about to founder upon sputtering trumpet tones, which its formulation obviously had not contemplated, and Tor and his trumpet banished to the hills.

This crisis was averted when Tor's startling rate of improvement quickly converted his detractors to enthusiastic admirers. His strident, wheezy blasts softened, became mellifluous, began to form soaring, lilting musical phrases, and Forzon, who had been indifferent to the trumpet's possible corruption of the country's technology was seized with deep concern over its inevitable impact upon Kurrian music. At first the ex-*torril* player labored incessantly to fit his trumpet tones into the inflected pentatonic scale employed by the *torril*. The trumpet stubbornly persisted in producing a natural overtones series. Finally, as Tor began to master the instrument, he stopped fighting its peculiarities and began to make use of them, and he started creating a surprisingly idiomatic music for trumpet. This he notated in a weirdly cryptic script that made no sense to Forzon even when he followed the music as Tor played.

119

The metalsmiths built trumpets for themselves, for their neighbors, for anyone who wanted one, and soon there were half a hundred enthusiastic trumpeters sending up shattering reverberations from all parts of the village, with more taking up the instrument as fast as the metalsmiths could turn them out. This unblending cacophony carried up the hill to the home of the king's agent, who paid one of his rare visits to the village to find out what was happening. His initial bewilderment gave way to disgust when he noted the number of inmates who had abandoned productive labor for trumpeting, and anger when it occurred to him that the village's stock of valuable metal, hitherto employed in the manufacture of useful and artistic objects for the enrichment of the king and himself, was being squandered on trumpets. Forzon, scenting trouble, made anxious inquiries, and the elders assured him that the village had the right to use its metal in whatever way it chose.

He began to make plans for a trumpet band. Concerted music was alien to native custom; by the time Cultural Survey came to Kurr the great tradition of Kurrian music might be altered beyond recognition, but it had to be done.

Nearly a month passed before the disappearance of Ann Cory occasioned a ripple of excitement in the village. Because of the custom of strict individual privacy, days went by before anyone suspected her absence. Eventually her quarters were examined, her unused clothing issue studied, cautious inquiries made as to when she had last been seen, and the governors reached the reluctant conclusion that their latest female arrival was missing.

The entire village turned out to search the surrounding countryside. As an elder sadly explained to Forzon, most one-handed people were able to accept life in a one-hand village, and in time even become happy there. But it did happen that the severance of an arm inflicted a deeper wound, and a weak person might turn to death as the only

120

cure. And of course it was always possible that the woman had met with an accident.

Forzon diligently joined in the search, and when, after several days, no trace of the woman had been found, the governors returned to their counsels and life in the village went on as before – with trumpets.

For uncounted generations the arts of Kurr had been family monopolies. Only the son of an artist could learn painting; only the son of a musician could study music. Forzon had not fully realized the extent to which such a tradition could be a deprivation to a passionately artistic and musical people, and the avidity with which the villagers took to the trumpet astonished him.

Here was a new musical instrument that had no family tradition. Anyone could play! One wanted only a teacher, and Tor, a great musician, was eager for pupils. The entire village responded. Work was neglected. The metal workers produced only trumpets.

On the next reckoning day the village's stock of crafted goods was so low that many of the wagons departed empty. The king's agent had a stormy conference with the village governors. Those worthy individuals were stubbornly and courageously adamant in their insistence on the villagers' traditional right of independence, but the incident left Forzon in a thoughtful mood.

'We do not want the displeasure of the king's agent,' he said to Tor. 'Only the best musicians should occupy themselves with music during the time for work. The others should perform their usual duties, and make music when their tasks are completed.'

'The king's agent has no right to interfere, but we shouldn't incur his anger needlessly,' Tor agreed. 'I will see that only the best musicians occupy themselves with music.'

'Your best musicians are attaining a high degree of skill. What are you going to do with them?'

'They shall continue to play music. What else is there to do with them?'

'Music exists to be heard,' Forzon said. 'When your trumpeters have sufficient skill and confidence you must take them to Kurra.'

Tor raised his hand in horrified protest. 'We would not dare!'

'There's no law against it,' Forzon said gently. 'There is no law that restricts us to a one-hand village. We are here only because we could not live elsewhere. It would be different with the trumpeters. Those who love music would welcome them, and all of Kurr loves music.'

'No one would listen!'

'Can people help listening if music is played for them? This wonderful new music you are making should not perish unheard in a one-hand village. You *must* go to Kurra!'

'We would not dare.'

'You cannot lose your left hand twice,' Forzon persisted.

'No. We would not dare.'

Forzon did not minimize the potential dangers that would await the trumpeters in Kurra. King Rovva, if they encountered him in a foul mood, was quite capable of innovation: those who had already lost an arm could easily lose their heads. Nevertheless, if the one-handed infamy were to be brought to an end the risk had to be taken. He would speak to Tor again.

Most of the would-be musicians returned to their normal tasks. The king's agent was not satisfied, however; he took to prowling the village and soon identified the individual responsible for the plague of trumpet music. He never spoke to Forzon, but Forzon encountered him with such frequency that he felt spied upon.

Eventually it dawned upon Forzon that the agent's attention had been attracted by his idleness. Other villagers did nothing, but they kept to themselves and did not flaunt their

122

sloth where it might corrupt the industrious. Forzon did nothing not just conspicuously, but with an intolerable enthusiasm. He enjoyed watching others work, he interrupted them with questions, he diverted their efforts to tasks of his own devising that were manifestly unlikely to profit the agent.

Clearly the agent considered him a corruptive influence that bore watching. Forzon, seated at his table lost in thought, would suddenly become aware of the agent's eyes at his window. As he lounged in the street, enthralled by the music of Tor's trumpeters – Tor had evolved a harmonic structure that Forzon thought unique – he would find the agent at his elbow, regarding him with sullen disapproval. Forzon could only hope that he was suspected of nothing more than being a bad influence, and after some days he found an easy solution: he went to work. He became a carpenter's helper. The king's agent observed and went away satisfied.

Of an evening, when Tor sat before his quarters massaging his weary embouchure, Forzon would say to him, 'Music exists to be heard.' And Tor would reply, 'We would not dare!'

Forzon lost his job on the third day. He was raptly admiring the beautiful grain of the tabletop they were fashioning and absently got his hand in the way of a chisel stroke. The cut was superficial, but it left the carpenter badly shaken. In a one-hand village no one wanted to be responsible for an injury to a hand. For a few days Forzon suffered the inconvenience of a bandage, and when the hand healed the carpenter was unaccountably unable to find any work for him. He moved down the street to the metal shop; his friends there had caught up with the demand and were no longer building trumpets, and they seemed hopeful that he might think of another project for them. He watched them work and helped when they needed an extra hand, always keeping in reserve a few menial tasks so that he could look busy if the king's agent came around.

And every evening he talked with Tor.

'Music exists to be heard.'

'We would not dare!'

It was mid-morning. The metalsmiths had just put the finishing touches on a set of matched bowls, and Forzon carried them to the storage shelf and then stepped into the street to enjoy a few moments of relaxing music and marvel again at the iron endurance of Tor's trumpeters. They were entering upon their third hour of rehearsal. The composition was new; Tor had discovered the fanfare and was making dazzling use of it. The tones carried brilliantly through the crisp fall air.

Forzon no longer feared for Kurr's musical tradition. Instead of destroying it the trumpet opened up a new dimension. The *torril* players would ignore trumpet music – Tor was certain of that; and this new music that Tor was creating, in an alien musical system and for an alien instrument, was uniquely Kurrian.

A new musical tradition was in the making, a tradition of one-handed trumpeters. Tor had already sent out a few of his musicians to find other one-hand villages and introduce the trumpet to them. It suited Forzon's plans, but however much he argued that though trumpet *playing* might properly be a monopoly of the one-handed, trumpet *listening* should be open to everyone, he made no headway.

The music cut off abruptly. Puzzled, Forzon strolled down the street to the village square. There the king's agent was talking quietly with the governors. Nearby, in ominous array, stood a full company of king's soldiers. The conference broke up almost at once, and the governors separated and began making the rounds of the village, asking all of the residents to come to the square.

'What does he want?' Forzon asked one of them.

'To speak to us,' the elder answered indifferently.

'It is about the work output? Surely he knows that he'll have full loads next time.'

'He hasn't said what it is about.'

The villagers assembled slowly. Forzon, tense with apprehension, found their indifference bewildering. They had been asked to come; they came, but not until they could conveniently put aside their tasks of the moment. The king had already inflicted his worst upon them, and here in their own village of living dead they thought themselves safely beyond his reach.

The agent, standing on a cart and scowling impatiently out over the gathering crowd, perspired freely under the warming sun and finally removed his outer garment. Forzon perspired and did not dare remove his.

Finally the governors signaled that the village was assembled.

'In the full moon of the third month past,' the agent shouted, 'a woman came to this village. She came, and then she vanished. Do any of you know of her or where she went?'

The crowd was silent.

'We have examined the king's records,' the agent went on, 'and we find that no woman has merited punishment since the second month of the old harvest. No woman suffered the loss of a hand, no woman was sent to this village, and yet a one-handed woman came here. You are warned to speak now if you know of her.'

He paused, looking searchingly out over the crowd. Forzon's mind hung numbly upon one word.

Records.

Team B had not known that the king kept records.

'Very well,' the agent continued. 'We have examined the king's records and the records of all of the one-hand villages, and we find that one of them is harboring a man who did not merit punishment. If he is here I order him to step forward.' Again he looked searchingly at the crowd. 'Very well,' he snapped. 'All those who arrived at this village between the harvests are ordered to step forward.'

To hold back would have been fatal. Forzon allowed

himself to be jostled forward with the others, and the king's soldiers moved to surround them.

'Search them!' the agent commanded.

Forzon had no time to react. It happened too quickly – his outer garment jerked away, the soldier's startled exclamation when the dummy stub of a left arm came with it, Forzon quickly stripped to the waist and his hidden arm bared to view.

The agent leaped from the cart and strode toward him. He stared at Forzon, passed a hand over his shaven head, stared again, and then fumbled in his garments to produce a portrait. He compared Forzon's profile with the copy of his ID photo and uttered a grunt of satisfaction.

'So!' he exclaimed. 'So you wish to live in a one-hand village!' He threw back his head and laughed gleefully. Greed sparkled in his eyes. No doubt the rewards offered for the capture of Supervisor Jef Forzon had been substantial. 'So you wish to live in a one-hand village,' the agent said again. 'I promise that the king will grant your wish – after he has discussed certain matters with you.'

Forzon was hoisted into the cart. Already the villagers were drifting away, but he managed to catch the eye of one of the governors as the cart began to move. 'Tell Tor,' he shouted, 'that music exists to be heard.'

A few minutes later the village lay behind them, and the cart was bumping over the rough track that led up out of the valley. Above its uneven creaking Forzon thought he caught the sound of music. Looking back at the village square, he could see the glint of the sun on rows of raised trumpets.

The musicians had returned to their rehearsal.

TWELVE

They proceeded only as far as the king's garrison, where a tent-like enclosure was quickly erected over the cart. Forzon sat inside with his hands and feet bound as Ann Cory's had been bound when he rescued her and reflected that he was about to be taught patience. Time passed, the cart remained motionless, and the tent became swelteringly hot; the king's agent and the garrison commander had drawn aside to engage in a vehement and interminable argument.

Finally the cart moved off, and its creaking drowned out their voices. Much later when Forzon was given a rest stop he found both of them marching with his escort, dust-stained, stonily silent.

'Cheer up!' he told them. 'Perhaps there will be reward enough for two.'

They glared at him.

He asked them to leave a flap open for ventilation; scornfully they laced the tent shut, and the cart creaked and bumped onward through the waning afternoon. Night brought coolness and a dim flicker of light from the torch a soldier was carrying ahead of the *esg*. Forzon toppled backward onto the hard boards and attempted to rest; he already knew that the rough road and the incessant, squalling racket made sleep impossible. Toward morning they reached the next garrison, where he was released briefly and allowed to eat.

Dawn came, and a flood of sunlight, and still they refused to allow him an inch of ventilation. 'Why not?' he demanded, and they would not answer.

He knew the answer. The king feared Team B and reasoned that if Forzon were brought to Kurra openly, the ubiquitous IPR agents would certainly learn of his capture and somewhere along the way effect his release.

The king was wiser than he knew. So confident had Team B been of Forzon's safety that it had left him isolated. By the time it got around to attempting another contact with him, Supervisor Jef Forzon would be beyond any assistance that Team B could offer.

The cart creaked and bumped forward, hour after hour, day after day, and Forzon learned patience. He knew when they reached Kurra because the irregular bumps of the road abruptly changed to an even jolting over paving stones. At length the cart stopped, and close behind it the crash of a closing gate rang out in the sudden silence.

A soldier reached in to untie Forzon's bonds. Forzon attempted to climb out, his numbed limbs gave way, and he was saved from a bad fall only by the soldier's panicky grab. The agent and the garrison commander snarled in unison; Forzon suppressed a smile. For the moment, at least, his health was valuable to someone.

Flanked by soldiers who half-carried him whenever his legs faltered, Forzon was moved quickly through a maze of corridors and ramps where daylight never penetrated, their long stretches of gloom feebly punctuated by tapers in wall brackets. In the upper reaches of the castle they halted before a wide doorway. A squad of sentries in the uniform of the king's personal guard took charge of Forzon, searched him diligently, and marched him into the room. The agent, the garrison commander, and Forzon's escort were left standing outside the door in shocked disappointment.

Feeling had slowly returned to Forzon's legs; he was able to stride forward boldly, but as they swept the length of the long room he experienced a crushing disappointment. Throughout his tedious journey the one thing he'd had to look forward to was a face to face confrontation with King Rovva – and the man on the high dais was not the king.

The guards executed a ritual bow, left foot forward, knee bending, and when they straightened up they turned on Forzon in indignation. 'Bow to your King's Minister!'

'He's not *my* King's Minister,' Forzon said mildly.

Swords were drawn; Forzon remained stubbornly erect.

'Seat him!' the Minister snapped.

Forzon was tied securely to a chair, and the guards repeated their bow and retreated half the length of the room. Forzon suppressed a smile. Whatever was spoken here would not be for the ears of underlings, which meant that King Rovva was still keeping knowledge of Team B from his people.

The Minister looked down at him stonily. A slender man with a worried, young-old face, he wore the ordinary street dress of the better class of Kurrian citizen. Too far below the nobility to merit royal robes but of a status so lofty it had no uniform, he had risen high enough to fall far, and he seemed nervously aware of that.

'Jef Forzon?' he demanded.

'That is my name,' Forzon said. 'Who are you?'

'Gasq, the King's First Minister.'

'I'm honored.'

Gasq regarded him with puzzlement. 'You are?'

'Is not an audience with the King's First Minister an honor in Kurr?'

Gasq scowled. 'Where is Paul Leblanc?'

'I haven't the faintest idea.'

The scowl deepened. 'When did you last see him?'

Desperate though Forzon's situation was, it had overtones of sheer hilarity. King Rovva had invested months of strenuous effort in capturing the man he considered the most important alien personage in Kurr, and Forzon knew less about Team B's activities than the most callow IPR trainee. The total import to the king of Forzon's whole knowledge would be a mere featherweight more than nothing at all. For that reason Forzon determined to tell the truth, with due moderation, until his captors were sufficiently convinced of his honesty to enable him to lie with effect.

He answered, 'I last saw Paul Leblanc before I left Kurra – before I went to the one-hand village.'

'*Where* did you see him?'

'I don't know the city well enough to tell you that. It was in a large apartment on the upper level of a building. From the windows it was possible to see over the city wall.'

'In what direction?'

Forzon pretended to deliberate. 'I don't know,' he announced finally. 'I'm afraid that the country surrounding Kurra would look very much the same to me in any direction.'

'Could you find this building again?'

'I doubt it. I went there at night; I left it hidden in a waggon. I didn't see much either coming or going, and it all happened a long time ago.'

'Where is Sev Rawner?'

'I haven't the faintest idea.'

'When did you see him last?'

'At the same time that I last saw Paul Leblanc. Wait!'

Gasq leaned forward eagerly.

'I saw him when I was leaving Kurra – when I was walking through the streets to the gate. I saw him from a distance, crossing a sidestreet.'

Gasq took a moment to master his disappointment. 'Where was he going?'

'I haven't the faintest idea.'

'Who was the woman who visited you at the one-hand village?'

'I knew her under the name of Ann Cory.'

'She has other names?'

'All Team B agents have several identities.'

'Where is Ann Cory now?'

'I don't know.'

'How many Team B agents are there?'

'I never saw a complete roster.'

'You are supervising coordinator of this world, and you don't know how many agents you have working for you?'

'Do you know the duties of an IPR supervising coordinator?' Forzon asked bluntly.

130

'No.'

'Neither do I.'

Gasq fell into the trap. He dropped the subject – which meant that Rastadt had given him a careful briefing on Cultural Survey Sector Supervisor Jef Forzon.

'What were you doing at the one-hand village?'

'Hiding,' Forzon said. 'Hiding until Team B could discover a way to get me out of Kurr.'

'Why did Ann Cory visit you?'

'To tell me that I'd have to remain there longer.'

There was more of it. Forzon readily identified the few agents he knew and described in detail what they were doing when he met them. He knew that Rastadt had already supplied such information; in any case, all of them had changed identities and appearance, and even their ID photos would be of small use to Gasq.

Finally Gasq signaled the guards forward. They untied Forzon, and he got leisurely to his feet.

'Your answers are not satisfactory,' Gasq announced. 'Among the King's loyal servants are many who are skilled in persuading prisoners to speak the truth. Next time you shall meet them.'

As Forzon turned away he noticed high up on the wall a window that looked down into the room where he stood. Seated there was a rotund figure enveloped in robes – King Rovva. For a moment their eyes met, Forzon returning the king's gaze boldly.

Then the guards performed their bow and moved Forzon away.

As they marched toward the door Forzon took the measure of his surroundings. The castle had been built at a time when Kurrian architects had become aware that two of the curving trees could be placed to form an arch, and they chose to flaunt their knowledge in this huge audience chamber. The place bristled with ornamental arches that curved over the room like fleshless ribs of a long-dead giant. The vault of the roof loomed far above them, dimly crossed

131

with the arches' shadows. Tapers in brackets lined one side of the room; on the other, Forzon was able to catch glimpses of the vast square before the castle and of the buildings beyond through jagged window slits.

The agent and the garrison commander were still waiting eagerly outside the door. 'Such a pity,' Forzon murmured, with mock solicitude. 'You should have collected your reward before I was interviewed.'

After another wild meandering through the maze of corridors he was shown into his quarters. He expected a dungeon; he received a room more appropriate to a guest of honor than a prisoner, large, lavishly furnished, but none the less a prison. The heavy door shut with a clang, a bar was rammed home, and he was left alone.

The room's window slits looked out onto an enclosed courtyard far below. He examined them and quickly satisfied himself that no period of self-enforced starvation would enable an adult to escape there. He turned to the zigzag slash in the thick door; his eyes met those of a guard, and other guards stood nearby in the quaint crouch that passed for military posture in Kurr.

'Obviously I won't lack for attention,' Forzon told himself, and began to feel less cheerful. Even if Team B found out where he was, he doubted that it could get him out.

Darkness came on. For a time Forzon amused himself with watching the guards walk their beats around the perimeter of the courtyard. Each carried a torch; the lights marched toward each other, wheeled, marched to meet other lights. The beats seemed very complicated.

Tiring of that, Forzon stretched out on his bed and thought about King Rovva. This was no pipsqueak handed a crown by accident of birth. The Team B agents had given Forzon a picture of a crafty man, cruel, capricious, self-indulgent, but with a refined instinct that checked every evil impulse short of an extreme that might serve to turn his subjects against him. Forzon read his character differently. This was an old man, and if he had not been blessed with

132

wisdom he had acquired it; and now he was deeply troubled. His tidy universe had been knocked askew. He was the evil product of an evil system, but Forzon reminded himself that the Kurrians were a profoundly decent people – and King Rovva was a Kurrian. He did what he did not through inherent cruelty but as a matter of the right with which the kings of Kurr were endowed.

Before Team B could turn the people against the king, it would have to turn him against himself. To catch the conscience of the king – that was the problem. And Team B had misunderstood it completely because no one in Team B believed that the king had a conscience.

The occupant of the next room began to moan and whimper. Forzon went to the window slits and attempted to attract his attention with hisses and whispers but got no response. He returned to his bed. The moans and sobbing continued, but the long journey had left Forzon exhausted and he fell asleep and slept soundly.

It was late morning when he awoke. He was given food, and then there was nothing for him to do but stand at the window slits and watch the guards parade in the courtyard below. He ruefully concluded that his lessons in patience were likely to continue indefinitely.

The sobbing and whining began again in the next room. Forzon went to the door and called to a guard, 'What is wrong with the person next door?'

The guard shrugged but did not answer. Forzon had been treated with almost studious politeness, but his guards would not speak to him.

'I'd like to have my quarters moved,' Forzon said. 'The noise disturbs me.'

The guard shrugged again, but a moment later there was a banging on the next door and a shouted command, and the sobbing stopped.

Later they returned Forzon to the audience chamber. Again he boldly strode the length of the room, and this time he ceremoniously executed the ritual bow.

133

Gasq stared at him. 'You bow? Why?'

'Excellency,' Forzon said, 'I erred. The bow is a custom of your people, and it was rude of me not to respect it. A gracious visitor should willingly adhere to the manners of his hosts. I apologize for my error, and correct it.'

Gasq absently signaled to the guards, who tied Forzon to the chair and withdrew. 'Why is Team B not leaving Kurr?' Gasq asked suddenly.

'Why should it leave?' Forzon asked, speaking directly to the king, who sat motionless in his observation window.

'Its rules require that it leave,' Gasq persisted. 'Its headquarters has ordered it to leave. Why does it not leave?'

Forzon kept his eyes on the king. 'Your Majesty is better informed than I am. I know little about Team B's rules, and nothing about its orders.'

'When the woman came to see you at the one-hand village, did she not tell you of these orders?' Gasq asked.

'Nary a word.'

'You are the supervising coordinator. You have the authority to order Team B to leave Kurr.'

'I have,' Forzon agreed.

'Why do you not do it?'

'I don't know where Team B is, and my present position seems to be one of receiving orders, rather than giving them.'

Smiling, he met the king's eyes boldly. Rovva's aspect was that of a profoundly puzzled man. He had the fugitive he had so desperately wanted, and he did not know what to do with him. For a second time he was weighing all of the evidence, and he remained undecided.

Gasq continued through the list of the same questions he'd asked previously, Forzon gave the same answers, and finally Gasq dismissed him.

His neighbor's incessant whimpering kept him awake that night, but Forzon hesitated to complain again. The suffering was too sharply reminiscent of that which Tor had endured. He finally drifted into a troubled sleep, and some time during the night his guards jerked him from his bed.

King Rovva had finally made up his mind.

The guards roughly hauled Forzon from the room. He went without protest, stumbling sleepily, and as they stepped into the corridor a shrill scream shattered the silence.

'Forzon!'

The guards rushed him away, but not before he had time to glance at the door slits of the next room. A face peered out at him, ghostly white in the flickering taper light.

His whining neighbor had been Coordinator Rastadt.

THIRTEEN

This time it was a dungeon.

From the concealing darkness came shrieks and moans and nauseous stench. The guard nudged Forzon roughly and kicked a rope ladder into a vast, circular pit. Menaced by a spear, Forzon obediently began to climb down. When he reached the end the guard laughed raucously and prodded with the spear, and Forzon descended hand over hand until he hung suspended from the lowest rung. Just as he was steeling himself for a long drop his toes touched. The ladder was jerked away, and Forzon found himself in inky darkness.

He looked up and caught his breath. The lofty ceiling was supported by enormous pillars that flared like the exterior walls of houses. Pillars, walls, ceiling – every place the light from the guards' torches touched glowed with swirling color. Never in his wildest imaginings could he have conceived of such a dungeon. Its sheer beauty overwhelmed him.

Guards strolled by at irregular intervals, their torches fleetingly lighting the pit as they passed. Forzon was able to pick out the figures of other prisoners asleep on damp, mouldy piles of straw. Tiny, evil-looking rodents scurried about unhindered, their large, luminous eyes flashing red when the light struck them. Forzon gathered some unoccupied straw, kicked it into a pile, and glumly sat on it to contemplate his foul surroundings.

He wanted to think about Rastadt, but he could not concentrate. The incessant moaning and sobbing of the prisoners was broken only by sudden shrieks and the unnerving, tremulous cries of the tortured damned. The rodents ran boldly across Forzon's feet. Whenever he absently breathed through his nose the potent stench made his stomach churn.

Rastadt's pale, pleading face haunted him. Obviously some falling out among thieves had delivered him into the king's hands, and Team B should be notified. With Rastadt no longer in control of base an immediate change of strategy was imperative.

And Rastadt—

He could not concentrate. Neither could he sleep. The wall of the pit oozed water; the straw was so damp that his clothing soaked through wherever he came in contact with it. He lurched to his feet and began pacing in a tight circle around his pile of soggy straw. He spoke to a passing guard, and the only response was a spear thrust that drew blood from his shoulder. When a neighbor awoke flailing in the throes of a nightmare Forzon attempted to talk with him, and the guard returned with a large crock and drenched both of them with slop.

Finally dawn sent shafts of light through slits high up on the walls. The effect was breathtaking. A strange, crystalline stone faced the walls and ceiling, and it broke the light into myriads of colors. Not even a people passionately fond of beauty would lavish so much of it on a dungeon. Perhaps this had once been the royal natatorium, a room filled with sparkling pools where the king cavorted with his harem. Now the pools were foul pits, and though beauty flashed far above few eyes were uplifted to see it.

The prisoners slowly dragged themselves from their tormenting dreams into tortured reality. A guard passed by and carelessly dumped food into the pit. Forzon watched with horror as prisoners and rodents clawed for it.

The chief guard, a handsome, effeminate-looking man with the graceful movements of a ballet dancer, passed through at midday taunting the prisoners. He paused to grin down at Forzon. 'So you're another one that won't talk.'

'I'm one who has nothing to say,' Forzon answered.

'You'll have plenty to say when they go to work on you. Met the black box yet?'

'I don't believe I've had that pleasure.'

The chief guard laughed shrilly. 'Pleasure? The black box'll give you plenty of pleasure, if that's what you want to call it. First it removes the nails from your left hand – one each day, so the pleasure'll last longer. If you still haven't anything to say, then it goes to work on your fingers – but just one joint of one finger at a time. The box is never in a hurry. Doesn't do anything fast, like cut. It just pulls – nails, finger joints, hand, forearm. It's versatile, too. If you won't talk after that, it can do the same with your right arm – and that *would* give us a problem. If a man had *both* arms removed, is he still eligible for residence in a one-arm village? It isn't for me to decide, but I've always wondered. Fortunately it rarely happens. A few finger joints are enough to convince most. They're glad enough to tell what they know and have the job finished with a sword. Take my advice, fellow. The sooner you do your talking and get started for a one-hand village, the better it will be for you.'

'I doubt it,' Forzon said. 'You see – I just came from a one-hand village.'

The chief guard regarded him speechlessly, several times looking from one of Forzon's hands to the other. He stomped away; a moment later one of the guards came and drenched Forzon with slop.

Then they started taking the prisoners. Throughout that

gruesome day the pathetic creatures were hauled off one at a time, wailing and pleading, and returned unconscious or sobbing convulsively, blood dripping from the rags that hid their mutilated left hands. When darkness finally put a stop to the outrages, Forzon succumbed to nervous exhaustion and managed a few hours of restless, hallucinatory sleep.

At dawn on the second day the guards took Forzon.

He went not so much in fear as in indignation. Among any people there would be moral degenerates who naturally gravitated to a service that allowed full scope to their sadistic impulses. The dungeon guards and the calloused manipulators of the black box might be only the diseased dregs of an otherwise healthy society.

Or they might not, in which case Forzon's notion about catching the king's conscience had to be written off as a naive illusion.

In a room off the dungeon the guards drenched Forzon with clean water and tossed him a change of clothing.

'Are your torturers too fastidious to work on a dirty prisoner?' he demanded.

He dressed himself, and they hustled him to the courtyard, bound his hands and feet, and placed him in an enclosed cart that immediately lurched off to creak its way through the streets of Kurra.

They passed a city gate, moved a short distance over the jolting ruts of a dirt road, and halted. After an interminable, sweltering delay the covering was removed, the cart wheeled about, and Forzon rode back through the city gate.

In the open.

The rashness of the move, following the king's astuteness in having him brought to Kurra in concealment, dumbfounded him – but only momentarily.

It was a trap. Before the king's black box removed Forzon's left arm one joint at a time and rendered him unfit for public display, he was being used as bait. Thus hauled

138

slowly through the streets with no apparent escort, someone from Team B would see him, there would be a rescue
attempt – and the king's ruffs would be waiting.

They were everywhere, clothed in civilian dress to mingle
with the thronging pedestrians, looking down from over-
hanging windows, gathered strategically at intersections. He
could not identify them, but he knew that they were there.
The plodding pace of the *esg* was so slow that they could
easily move their trap along with it. His only visible escort
consisted of four men in the uniform of the king's grooms,
but those pedestrians who so diligently kept pace with the
cart had to be ruffs, and directly ahead and behind came
enclosed wagons that undoubtedly contained passengers.
The cunning of the thing was diabolical. Even the creaking
din of the vehicles seemed a part of the conspiracy. Forzon
could have screamed warnings all the way to the castle
without being heard.

Their route spiraled through the city, following narrow
byways that could easily be blocked off. Up ahead the ruffs
were keeping the way clear of other vehicles. Forzon sat
immobile, perspiring, weak with dread and anger, searching the passing throngs of familiar faces and hoping desperately that he would not find them.

A slender tradesman looked up from a customer to
glance disinterestedly at the passing cart. Joe Sornel, the
ex-pourer? Forzon quickly turned away. A husky pedes-
trian stared at Forzon for a moment and then moved on,
pushing forward with long strides to disappear around a
corner. Hance Ultman? Forzon attempted to mask his face
in the billowing cloak that concealed the bindings on his
hands and feet.

And nothing happened. They penetrated almost to the
inner city, bumping forward slowly with a groom clutching
the *esg's* ear to further retard the animal's plodding pace.
Forzon had a fleeting glimpse of a citizen entering a building. It looked like Leblanc. In these troubled times Leblanc
shouldn't be looking anything like Leblanc, but this man

had. A stooped, elderly man shuffled into the street just ahead of them, found himself under the nose of the *esg*, and bewilderedly scrambled out of the way. Sev Rawner without his cataracts? And the woman leaning from the upstairs window to call to someone across the way – did she have Ann Cory's turned up nose?

He was seeing Team B everywhere.

They turned, and far up ahead the narrow street opened onto the vast square before the castle. The groom tugging at the *esg's* ear had done his job too well; they fell behind the leading wagon, and suddenly a cart edged out of a courtyard just ahead of them, cutting in between and blocking their way. A groom leaped forward shouting angrily, and Forzon's cart came to a sudden halt.

Forzon twisted sideways, pushed with his feet, and toppled out of the cart.

He fell on a groom, who clutched him frantically. The other groom came running, there was a shouted order, and ruffs boiled into the street from all directions. The groom continued to hold Forzon in a vise-like embrace, as though his life depended on Forzon's not escaping. Probably it did. The ruffs pressed this way and that; the intruding cart driver tried to back up and found his way blocked by foot traffic. The ruffs ordered him back, ordered him ahead. He raised his hands bewilderedly, and they seized him and rushed him away.

Forzon was roughly flung back into the cart, where two grooms sat on him. He relaxed and breathed easily for the first time since the long ordeal began. He had seen no sign of Team B, and the king's trap was a shambles. Finally the cart began to move again, but Forzon was kept flat in the bottom until it had safely crossed the square and the portal of the castle courtyard had clanged shut behind it. About the courtyard, where previously there had been only a few bored sentries, soldiers stood watchfully in formation.

They took Forzon directly to Gasq. The king, looking down from his high window, seemed to have aged since

Forzon had seen him last. So had Gasq; he did not give Forzon time to bow before he blurted, 'Why did you fall from the cart?'

Forzon shrugged. 'I'd had a long ride, half of it in a stuffy, enclosed cart, and I've had nothing to eat since day before yesterday. I felt dizzy. Perhaps I fainted.'

The king, Forzon thought, was a more complex individual than either he or Team B had realized. This failure of a carefully contrived plan should have called forth the same rage that struck blindly at Tor, but it had not. Instead his reaction seemed calmly deliberative: the plan had failed, so he would devise other plans.

'Did you see anyone from Team B?' Gasq demanded.

'I *thought* I did,' Forzon answered, watching the king.

'You *thought*—'

Forzon smiled. 'You see – I don't know what the members of Team B look like.'

Gasq sputtered disbelievingly. You don't know—'

'I know what they looked like when I was last in Kurra, but they'll have changed their appearances. They are very skilled at that.'

'But you thought you saw some of them?'

'I saw two men who resembled Team B members I have met, but I'm certain it was only a coincidence. In my condition I may not have been seeing clearly. As I said, I've had nothing to eat since day before yesterday. Anyway, if the few members of Team B whom I know haven't changed their appearances, they will now. By parading me through the streets you've let Team B know that I'm a prisoner. Everyone who has had any contact with me will change. Every meeting place I've visited will be abandoned. That was a bad mistake you made, taking me through the city like that. Now I am no longer of any use to you.'

Obviously the mistake, if it was one, was Gasq's, and he well knew the fate of king's ministers who made bad mistakes. His face paled, and he snarled. 'I'll persuade you to be useful!'

As he signaled the guards forward, the king's voice boomed out, blurred and amplified freakishly by the room behind him. 'Why has he not eaten since day before yesterday?'

- Gasq looked stricken and did not attempt to answer.

'Bring food,' the king ordered.

Servants scurried into the room to lay a table for Forzon. A delay followed; the sudden command had taken the kitchen by surprise. The king left his window, and when the servants finally brought the food he followed them into the room and stood by the table while each servant bowed and offered his tray for inspection.

'Seat yourself and eat,' the king told Forzon.

Forzon bowed an acknowledgement and sat down. The king banished Gasq to the far end of the room with a gesture and calmly seated himself opposite Forzon. Forzon self-consciously sampled a circle of bread, found that he was as hungry as he had claimed, and began to eat. More trays were paraded before him. The makings of a feast gradually cluttered the tabletop. Not until Forzon had fully satisfied his hunger did the king speak.

Then he said softly, almost conspiratorially, 'You said that you wanted to leave Kurr.'

'In my position, wouldn't you want to leave Kurr?'

'You may leave,' the king said, 'if you will take Team B with you.'

'Team B is scattered all over Kurr,' Forzon said. 'I haven't any idea how to get in touch with it.'

'Could you if you were freed?'

'No. But if I were *really* free, perhaps Team B would get in touch with me.'

'And – you would then leave, and take Team B with you?'

Forzon hesitated, fearing that a lie would not be believed and that the truth might destroy the small progress he had made. 'I was wondering whether Team B would obey my order to leave,' he said, when the king stirred impatiently.

'Team B has its own sworn mission in Kurr. Do you know what it is?'

The king did not answer.

'It would be difficult to explain it to your satisfaction,' Forzon went on, 'but if you were to do one thing you would be much better able to understand it.'

'What one thing?'

'Spend a few days in your dungeon – as a prisoner.'

The stroke of anger Forzon half expected did not come. The king evidently regarded Supervisor Jef Forzon as an enigma to be solved, rather than as a prisoner to be put in his place. He cocked his head and regarded Forzon with a look of profound puzzlement.

Suddenly he leaped to his feet to stare toward the window slits. Behind Forzon a servant dropped a tray and no one noticed. The guards lost their poise, weapons drooped, heads turned, mouths opened. At the distant end of the room Gasq left off glaring in Forzon's direction to hurry in wonderment to the nearest window slit.

Floating across the city, clear and mellow, giving stir to a thousand glittering echoes, came the sound of trumpets.

FOURTEEN

For hours the trumpet music tossed about the rooftops of Kurra, but it could be heard only fitfully in the room to which Forzon was hastily removed when King Rovva banished him from mind and presence with an absent gesture. His window slits looked upon the same courtyard he had seen from his first castle room, but from a higher level. Soldiers still stood there in orderly ranks, presumably alert to an attempt to rescue Forzon. The king had forgotten them, though his trap was still set and baited.

Tor's trumpeters had lost none of their endurance. They

143

played until late afternoon, and it was long after they ceased when the castle routine finally returned to normal, the usual comings and goings could be heard in the corridor, loaded wagons entered the courtyard, the soldiers were dismissed, and someone finally remembered Forzon and brought food to him.

Darkness fell. Forzon watched the marching torches until boredom and his exhaustion from the sleepless nights in the dungeon and the long day of tension drove him to his bed.

He was awakened by an urgent hand and a whispered question. 'Supervisor?'

He grunted sleepily.

'Come! Quickly!'

He wrenched himself to alertness. His door stood open, admitting light from a bracketed taper in the corridor beyond, and the figure bending over him cast a huge shadow.

'Who is it?' Forzon whispered.

'Ultman. Had a devil of a time finding you, we're late, let's go.' He hissed into a pocket communicator, 'I've got him, clear out.' Then he moved off.

Forzon scrambled to his feet and followed.

Two guards lay unconscious on the corridor floor. Forzon regarded them compassionately as he stepped over their inert bodies. Before dawn they would be in the king's dungeon, destined for a meeting with the black box.

Ultman hurried along the dim corridor with long strides, and Forzon had to trot to keep up with him. At the first intersection they passed three more supine guards.

'Got to hurry,' Ultman panted. 'Only gave them a low charge.'

They turned onto a descending ramp and raced down it at top speed. At the bottom Ultman came to an abrupt stop, motioned Forzon back against a wall, and moved ahead to peer around a corner. He wore a uniform that Forzon did not recognize, with a hood that partially concealed his face, and his face . . .

144

Forzon gaped at him, gaped at an elderly, wrinkled face with a disfiguring bloat.

'Looks all right,' Ultman muttered. 'Wish I could have brought a cloak for you, but I couldn't risk it. Today the guards are suspicious of everything. We'll have to chance it. Come on.'

Forzon did not move. 'The coordinator,' he said.

'What about him?'

'I think he's on this level.'

'We'll settle with him later. Come on.'

'He's a *prisoner*!'

'*Rastadt?*'

Forzon nodded. 'At first they kept me on this level. I think it was this level. Rastadt was in the next room.'

'That's different.' Ultman pushed his hood back and pawed his hair fretfully. 'I've got to make the effort, I guess. After tonight *nobody* will get in or out of this place for months. Come on.'

They moved off side by side. At the first turning Ultman stopped and looked about thoughtfully. 'Do you know how to get to him?'

Forzon shook his head. 'All the corridors look alike to me. All I know is that the room overlooked the courtyard.'

'Which courtyard?'

'I didn't know there was more than one.'

'There are four. I'd better do this alone.' He cautiously opened a door and looked in. 'Storage room. Wait here. If I don't come back – take this.' He passed a coil of rope to Forzon. 'You'll be on your own. Try to find an outside window. If you can make it to the ground help will be waiting.'

The door closed, leaving Forzon in darkness. Time passed; he began to finger the rope nervously.

Abruptly the door jerked open. 'Hurry!' Ultman hissed. Rastadt was stumbling along the corridor toward them, moaning softly, his emaciated figure draped in a long black cloak.

'See if you can shut him up,' Ultman whispered irritably.

Forzon went to meet Rastadt, slipped an arm around him, tried to hurry him. Ultman ranged ahead of them, scouting out their route and dashing back at intervals to plead vainly for quiet and more speed. Rastadt's best gait was a tottering limp and no importunities could stop his moaning, which drew inquisitive sentries like a magnet. They continued to move haltingly, Ultman flashing a strange, buzzing hand weapon that left their meandering course strewn with unconscious guards. Even that faltering pace slowed relentlessly as Rastadt's enfeebled legs gave out. Forzon supported his weight as best he could and continued to urge him forward, but the moment came when the coordinator refused to take another step. Lolling helplessly, face wet with tears, he sobbed, 'Go away. Leave me alone.'

'We're almost there,' Ultman hissed. He turned, gave Rastadt's face a stinging slap, and snapped, 'Move!'

The coordinator staggered forward again. They rounded a corner; Ultman dispatched one more sentry and swore softly when the man threshed on the floor and attempted to get up. 'Charge gone,' Ultman announced, and clouted the sentry behind the ear with the weapon's butt. He flung open a door. 'Now if things aren't messed up outside—'

Forzon coaxed Rastadt into the room and closed the door behind them. Ultman had hurried to a narrow window. He flashed a light; an answering flash came from the darkness below. 'The rope!' Ultman hissed. 'We'll have to slide down.' He played it out, secured it, and turned to Rastadt. 'You first, Coordinator. Think you can make it?'

Rastadt emitted an agonized moan. 'I *can't.*'

Ultman turned the light on him, and Rastadt thrust aside his cloak and held up both arms.

He had no hands.

Without a word Forzon pulled up the rope and tied it around Rastadt's chest, under his arms. Together they lowered the coordinator. Considering his former robustness he seemed pathetically light, but the rope was slender and cut and burned cruelly whenever it slipped through their hands.

Finally it went slack. Ultman nudged Forzon, who scrambled through the window. The rope tore at his hands as he plummeted downward, fighting to slow his descent with his feet. He struck the ground with a jolt that numbed his legs and sent him sprawling; Ultman was just behind him and sprawled on top of him. Eager hands pulled both of them erect, and Ultman performed a sleight of hand trick with the rope, jerked it free, and coiled it up as they hurried away. High above them the castle windows were a blaze of light. The search was on.

Rastadt had already been carried off. A firm hand guided Forzon through the night, steering him around the inert forms of fallen guards. They angled across the vast square and overtook those carrying the coordinator as they gained the row of buildings on the opposite side.

A door opened and closed silently behind them. Someone pushed Forzon into a lighted room and thumped him resoundingly on the back. The voice was that of Joe Sornel, the ex-pourer; the unhandsome face was unrecognizable, but any face possessed of that voice would have been to Forzon a thing of beauty.

'We brought it off!' Joe exulted.

'That weapon of Ultman's is a handy gadget,' Forzon observed.

Joe nodded. 'Stun-gun. We don't like to use them, but this was sort of an emergency.'

'You have no idea how much of an emergency it was!'

'Want to bet?' Joe asked grimly. 'What the devil went wrong? We thought you were enjoying a nice, safe vacation, and suddenly Hance comes busting in to say the king's got you.'

Forzon dropped into a chair and accepted a mug of *cril* that someone thrust at him, and when he had caught his breath somewhat and drained the mug, he described the

147

turmoil set in motion by Ann's disappearance.

Joe lifted both hands wearily. 'Dames! She's supposed to stay there and help you work out your plan. Instead she comes trooping back and says you got no plan and won't never have no plan and all you want to do is walk in the meadow and smell the pretty flowers. Nuts! But maybe it's just as well. We got Rastadt!'

'Where is he?' Forzon asked, looking about.

'They took him out through the tunnel. He's in a bad way, and being as he has to be carried we thought it best to get him as far away as possible before the ruffs come calling. The rest of us can scramble if we have to.'

'Is Leblanc around?'

'He went with Rastadt. Hey – we'll have to do something about those hands. Did you bleed like that all the way over here? Lon, the supervisor left a blood trail!'

Lon hurried off to check; Joe spread a cooling ointment on Forzon's hands, and bandaged them, and then he sat back with a grin to ask, 'What goes with the trumpets?'

'Didn't Ann tell you about them?'

'Nary a word. We didn't know a thing until this afternoon – yesterday afternoon – when a bunch of one-handed guys turned up in the south market. Cleared it out completely when they marched in. Everyone left, and came storming back the moment they started to play. Coins rained for twenty minutes after the first number. What have you got up your sleeve?'

Forzon regarded his bandaged hands thoughtfully. 'Arms,' he said. 'Two of them, complete with appendages, for which I am profoundly grateful.'

'Playing it that way, eh? We were too busy getting ready to spring you to give the trumpeters much thought, but like I told Paul when they started to play, if trumpets is what it takes to give Kurr a democracy, no wonder IPR never made any progress here. It'd be four *thousand* years before anyone in IPR thought of trumpets. Find anything, Lon?'

'No,' the other IPR agent said. 'He couldn't have bled

148

much. But there's torches coming. Spreading out in all directions. They'll hit every house.'

Joe grunted disgustedly. 'They're not waiting for morning. Bring your mug, Supervisor. Lon doesn't want the ruffs finding evidence that he's had visitors. You can leave it in the tunnel. Luck, Lon. See you tomorrow – maybe.'

He led Forzon down to the tunnel.

They followed a complicated route reminiscent of the one taken on the night of the blowup. Forzon, emerging from the fifth tunnel, said awesomely, 'Did they carry the coordinator through this?'

'They had plenty of help,' Joe said. 'There are shortcuts, but of course they couldn't risk them carrying the coordinator. The ruffs will really be buzzing tonight. You'll have to stay off the streets yourself until your hands heal.'

'And my hair grows out?' Forzon suggested.

Joe snorted. 'All that needs is a wig, and you can have your choice of a couple of hundred hair styles.'

Leblanc was waiting for them at their destination, another subcellar with a concealed entrance. The Team B commander was no longer an elderly gentleman farmer. His hair was thicker and darker, he wore the dress of a common laborer and his face had miraculously acquired a matching coarseness. He absently gripped Forzon's bandaged hands, uttered a startled apology, and examined them with concern. 'It's good to see you, Supervisor,' he said. 'We made a serious miscalculation. I'm glad it didn't turn out worse.'

'How's the coordinator?' Forzon asked.

'Ill. Very ill, both physically and mentally.' He sighed. 'These things happen. I know I'm not responsible in this case, but I keep thinking of how easily it could have been prevented. He wants to see you. It won't be a pleasant experience. Do you feel up to it?'

Forzon nodded.

Leblanc opened a door and stood waiting, and Forzon walked toward the pallet where the coordinator lay. For a long time Rastadt was unaware of his presence. Finally he turned, met Forzon's eyes. 'Thank you,' he said, and burst into tears.

Leblanc quietly drew Forzon away. In the next room he got him seated, poured a bowl of wine for him, and announced soberly, 'We've made a terrible mistake.'

'In what way?' Forzon asked.

'Rastadt has been a prisoner since the night you two landed in Kurr.'

'You mean – the ambush on the coast—'

Leblanc nodded. 'He was captured and brought to Kurra under wraps, and he's been a prisoner ever since. They tortured him. Horribly.'

'But you had messages from him after—' Forzon straightened up suddenly, spilling his wine. '*Wheeler*!'

'Yes. Wheeler, curse his rotten soul. It was he who gave you the wrong language, dressed both of you in Larnorian costume, picked a landing place where Team B was least likely to find out about it – and tipped off the king's men that you were coming. With both of you captured – he thought – he took control of base and signed Rastadt's name to messages. And when finally he learned that you were safe he tried to destroy Team B to cover up his treachery.'

'I see.'

'Rastadt was simply a man far gone in senility who'd lost control of his command. Wheeler has been his assistant for years. He was a good assistant – too good. He made Rastadt's reputation for him, and Rastadt relied on him completely. I suppose – I don't know what I suppose. That it rankled to be doing work another man got the credit for, but that couldn't account for *this*.' He shook his head. 'It was Wheeler who meddled in Team B's affairs – in Rastadt's name – and the coordinator never knew about it. He knew almost nothing about Kurr, and very little about Larnor, which was why Wheeler was able to hoodwink him so completely. You too, of course.'

'Wheeler must have corrupted a high percentage of the base personnel.'

'I'm afraid so.'

'But why? It doesn't make any more sense with Wheeler than it did with Rastadt.'

Leblanc said slowly, 'I don't know. I – don't – know.'

'They tried to force Rastadt to talk,' Forzon said. 'He couldn't have told them anything even if he'd been willing, because he knew so little. That was why he was tortured.'

Leblanc nodded, his face grave and pale.

'And that explains the king's peculiar conduct toward me,' Forzon went on. 'Torture didn't break Rastadt. Probably that never happened before in all the history of Kurr. When I said I knew nothing it gave the king pause. He'd subjected one IPR officer to the black box and gained only a maimed prisoner. It wasn't worth maiming me just to obtain the same result. He tried to think of a better use for me.'

'And thereby got you rescued,' Leblanc said with a chuckle. 'If he hadn't turned out his ruffs and paraded you through the streets, he could have held you indefinitely without our knowing about it.'

'And if the coordinator hadn't lost his hands, I certainly would have lost mine.'

Leblanc shrugged. 'What happened was his own fault, and yet I have to pity the man. He's suffered grievously for such a small offense as continuing to hold office when he was no longer capable of performing his duties. Grievously. But it's done, now, and you're both safe.' He squared his shoulders in the manner of a man who has work to do and wants to get on with it. 'Tell me about the trumpets.'

'What are you going to do about Wheeler?'

'Nothing. Follow the same plan you laid out when we thought it was Rastadt. Ignore him.'

'Have you had any communication with base?'

'Not since the message ordering us to pull out. We

simply turned everything off.' He shrugged. 'Nuts to Wheeler. He can't touch us. What about the trumpets?'

Forzon smiled and shook his head.

'I'm no CS man,' Leblanc said, 'but I thought they played darned well.'

'The Kurrians seem to be innately musical.'

'They like trumpet music. Everyone packed up when the trumpeters first arrived. Shops closed, the farmers tossed produce back onto their carts, citizens ran for cover, and the trumpeters stood there innocently as if it was no doing of theirs. Then they started to play, and by the time they finished their first number the market place was packed with people yelling their heads off and throwing money. A few weeks of this and your trumpeters will be independently wealthy. I'll have to admit that I don't see what you're aiming at.'

'It's supposed to be a scientific experiment,' Forzon said. 'The old saw about the irresistible force and the immovable object.'

'I *still* don't see—'

'You couldn't,' Forzon said. 'I don't see it myself. I'm afraid my irresistible force is pointed in the wrong direction, and I can't do anything about that because I don't know which one is which.'

FIFTEEN

There was no open space in Kurra large enough to contain everyone who wanted to hear the trumpets, so Tor, on the second day, astutely divided his musicians into five groups – four for the markets, and the fifth, the largest contingent, for the square before the castle. Watching one group from a window overlooking the south market, Forzon found to his amazement that Tor had somehow grasped the *visual* potentialities of trumpet music. His men wore flowing scarlet cloaks – the agent would have gnashed his teeth to see so much of the village's production of luxury cloth squandered – and they stood erect with trumpets at a high angle and put their gleaming instruments through a synchronized ballet of movement while they played. The pictorial effect was as stunning as the sound.

The crowd jamming the market place sent up a frenzy of ecstatic approval after every number, and even at a distance Forzon had to raise his voice to make himself heard. He said, 'Haven't the ruffs paid any attention to them?'

Joe Sornel grinned impishly. 'The ruffs got better things to do this morning. They're all out looking for *you*. Word is that fifteen castle guards will be on their way to a one-hand village as soon as they stop bleeding, and if the ruffs don't find you, like *fast*, the fifteen will have company. Relax. Your trumpet scheme is really clicking, and the ruffs haven't got time to interfere.'

'It's clicking too well,' Forzon said glumly.

Leblanc bounded into the room excitedly. The crowd had unleashed another frenzy of applause, and he waited, rubbing his hands with satisfaction, until the noise faded. 'I think I see the pattern,' he chortled. 'I just think maybe I see it. I don't suppose you'd want to tell me—'

'Tell you what?'

'Never mind. The king has ordered a special festival to feature your trumpeters.'

Forzon stared incredulously. 'The king has *what*?'

'Ordered a special festival. Let's go where we can talk.'

Forzon obediently followed him to the cellar, where music and applause reached them only faintly. 'The king has ordered a festival,' Leblanc said again. 'For tonight. Your trumpeters will be the star attraction. They'll probably draw a record crowd. Too bad you can't go.'

'I might as well tell you now,' Forzon said resignedly. 'My plan is a complete flop.'

'What did you expect would happen?'

'Not this. How much time do we have before Supreme Headquarters yanks us out of here?'

'No idea. Maybe forever. Now that I know that Wheeler is responsible for this mess, I doubt that Supreme Headquarters has been told anything at all. His announcement that the planet was blown was only a ruse to trap Team B. My hunch is that he wouldn't dare put that in a report, because sooner or later Supreme would send a force to pick up all IPR personnel, including him. You can count on that. And what happened next wouldn't be pleasant for Assistant-Coordinator Blagdon Wheeler.'

'He may have a way to beat it.'

'I don't see how he could.'

'One of the reasons Wheeler is so dangerous,' Forzon said, meeting Leblanc's eyes squarely, 'is because he's so easy to underestimate. If he does have a way to beat it, then he's probably turned in that report. Which means that we have very little time left.'

'How much time do you need?'

'Enough time to think of a new idea and start over.'

It was Leblanc's turn to stare. 'Is it the festival that's upset your plan? What did you expect? King Rovva is as fond of music and the arts as any of his subjects.'

'Much fonder,' Forzon said dryly. 'And that I hadn't counted on.'

Ann Cory brought their lunch. She was disguised as a young Kurrian housewife, which Forzon thought a vast improvement on her earlier disguises. She nodded without looking at him, passed him a bowl of Kurrian stew, and remarked quietly that the trumpet music was very pretty.

'What are you doing now?' Forzon asked her.

'Nothing,' she said. She crumbled bread for them, filled their *cril* mugs, heaped a bowl with fruit, and hurried away.

Leblanc left as soon as he finished eating, and when he had gone Joe said with a quiet chuckle, 'Ann has a guilty conscience, in addition to which Paul burned her good for

154

walking out on you. If she'd followed orders and stayed there no one would have counted noses and you'd have been safe indefinitely. Her playing the flighty dame could have cost you an arm, or worse. So she has that on her conscience, besides which Paul relieved her of her assignments and put her on kitchen duty.'

'She's too good an agent for kitchen duty.'

'Sure. But even a good agent has to follow orders, or we'd get nowhere. If you want to take her off the hook, though, just give her an assignment. You're boss here.'

'I don't know any assignments,' Forzon said. 'But tell her to take the evening off and go to the festival. Everyone else will.'

Joe grinned and went to deliver the message. He came back scowling. 'Dames! She says no thanks, she's already heard the trumpets. Want to make that an order?'

Forzon shook his head. 'Are you going to the festival?'

'Nope. Paul says you aren't to be left alone under any circumstances, and I'm elected. Anyway – I've already heard the trumpets, too.'

Forzon waited up with Joe, still holding a faint hope that something might be retrieved from the debacle; but those attending returned at midnight and reported that Tor's men had stopped the show. They opened the program, and when the audience refused to let them go they played the rest of the evening.

'Everyone in Kurra is talking about nothing but trumpet music,' Leblanc said. 'I've never seen such excitement. If you have any action in mind, this is the time. One of the city gates had no guards on it tonight. They must have gone AWOL to hear the music. What do you want us to do about it?'

'Nothing,' Forzon answered. 'I told you – it didn't work. Do *you* have a plan?'

'I?' Leblanc looked startled.

'So it's up to me,' Forzon said resignedly. 'And we haven't an inkling of how much time we have. I'll sleep on

155

it, and tomorrow we'll have a conference to see if anyone else has any ideas.'

He slept late on it. Toward noon Leblanc exploded into his room; in an instant Forzon was wide awake and scurrying for an escape panel. Leblanc hauled him back. 'You *wizard!*' he panted.

'What's the matter now?' Forzon demanded.

'The king has just delivered himself of an edict. No more trumpet music. All the trumpeters are ordered back to their one-hand village. Dire consequences are promised for anyone who blows a trumpet in a public place and as bad for anyone who listens. That's what you wanted, isn't it?'

Forzon nodded.

'But what the devil – why would the king – and just last night he *honored* them with a festival appearance!' Leblanc waved his arms perplexedly. 'What's the next move?'

'Send a message to Tor,' Forzon said. 'Give him greetings from the Giver of Trumpets. Tell him to march his men through the streets to the castle and petition the king.'

A building's architecture usually looked subtly different to Forzon after he had been inside, but the ponderous stone castle of Kurra remained simply ponderous. Actually the castle consisted of several large buildings connected together, and as Forzon studied it from across the square he suddenly understood something about Kurrian architecture that had been troubling him from the beginning.

It was a frozen art. The people's thinking about it was static.

It had evolved from curving trees to curving walls of wood houses and finally to a rigid standardization that required stone structures to be built with the same outward-flaring walls. In a castle these served a natural defensive purpose, but that hardly accounted for their use in every building in Kurr.

The country's political situation had been stable for centuries, its population was stable, its technology at a stand-

156

still. The quality of craftmanship was such that buildings lasted almost indefinitely. As a result few new structures were built, and those few were slavish imitations of the old, with an elaborate overlay of ornamentation.

The trouble with Kurrian architecture was that there were no architects. There was no work for them to do.

'Do you see something over there?' Leblanc asked.

'No,' Forzon said, keeping his eyes on the castle. 'I just made a discovery about Kurrian architecture. There are no Kurrian architects – only builders.'

He turned and found himself the focal point of a roomful of puzzled faces. 'How can you think about architecture at a time like this?' Leblanc demanded.

'How can you look at a building without thinking about architecture?' Forzon answered.

Already the square thronged with people. Amazingly, at least a quarter of them were women, and a story bruited about the city that morning had it that some women had attended the festival the previous night, disguised as men. Forzon's trumpets seemed to be producing an incidental revolution that he had not contemplated.

Children peered down curiously from all sides, many in windows but most of them congregated on the housetops. These were the peculiar domain of children in Kurra – they gamboled and slid about the curving roofs, and the connected buildings enabled them to range from one side of the city to the other over a playground completely invisible from the streets below. Fortunately there were no children in the square. When an irresistible force met an immovable object someone was likely to be hurt, and Forzon had hoped it wouldn't be children.

The news that the king had banned the trumpeters and that they were on their way to the castle had passed through Kurra like a sudden, violent wind that first chased the populace to cover and then brought it into the streets to talk about what had happened. Team B had been energetically rumor mongering, but its scant numbers could not have produced this instantaneous movement on the castle square. The only reason all of Kurra had not gathered there was because the square was not large enough. Streets opening into it were crammed with people as far back as Forzon could see, all of them vainly attempting to push toward the square.

The crowd was strangely silent. Studying it doubtfully from an upper-storey window, Forzon felt like an amateur chemist who had assembled some chemicals at random and attached a fuse. Now the fuse was burning, but when it reached the end he had no idea whether the materials he'd put together would explode or merely go out.

He knew far too little about these people. He thought he understood them, but understanding was important without knowledge. Team B possessed the knowledge and understood none of it. Together they might have succeeded if only they'd had sufficient time.

Leblanc said softly, 'The only time I can remember a crowd behaving like this one was on another world at the funeral of a state hero. Are they actually *mourning* the death of the trumpet music?'

'They're curious,' Ann said.

'But why are they so subdued?' Leblanc asked.

' "Awed" is the word,' Ann said. 'When was the last time anyone in Kurr petitioned a king about anything? I say they're awed, and they're curious.'

'You're wrong,' Forzon told her. 'They're incredulous – I hope.'

'Incredulous that anyone would dare to petition the king?'

'Incredulous that the king has banned the trumpeters. They don't want to believe it.'

'You hope,' Ann added dryly.

Forzon nodded. 'I hope.'

A distant sound of cheering reached them. White flashed in the square as every face turned. The trumpeters were coming.

They advanced with torturous slowness. People joggled and pushed back to form a narrow lane that snapped shut the moment they passed. They walked two abreast, red capes flapping, gleaming instruments held upright. Cheers followed them all the way across the square; but though the crowd continued to make way for them, their already tedious pace faltered perceptibly as they approached the castle.

They halted before the imposing facade, appearing at that distance like one short dash of scarlet in a sea of mixed colors. The hush of the crowd was death-like. Leblanc was watching with binoculars, and he whispered, 'I see the king. In the large central window. That's his reviewing stand on fete days.'

They heard nothing of Tor's petition – only an upwelling murmur of approval from the crowd around him when he had finished. The king apparently delivered a brief reply, but no sound of that reached across the square. Then the musicians turned and began to make their way back through the crowd.

The fuse had burned to the end, and Forzon could hear the figurative fffft. 'So it was a dud,' he said resignedly.

'Dud?' Leblanc exclaimed. 'Do you realize that this is the first time in four hundred years that we've managed so much as a public demonstration? What comes next?'

'I don't know. Unless—' Forzon leaned far out of the window and shouted at the top of his voice. 'Music!' Leblanc immediately echoed the word, screaming into Forzon's ear and so startling him that he nearly lost his balance. They shouted together, 'Music! Music!' The crowd below seized upon it, and in an instant it had swelled to a thundering, rhythmic crash that filled the square. 'Music! Music!'

The retreating trumpeters had reached the center of the square, their instruments still held erect. Forzon watched them tensely. Would they defy the king and play? They had to, if anything at all was to be salvaged from the demonstration. Were they wavering? Would Tor dare?

Across the square the castle gate swung open and the king's ruffs poured out. Flailing about them with swords and spears, they pushed into the crowd. For a moment the startled citizens gave way; then they turned with a roar and surged back to seize the ruffs, fling them to the ground, trample them. Captured weapons were flung defiantly at the castle windows. The crowd flowed toward the castle gate like a tidal wave, smashed it open and poured through. From the square, from the streets beyond, an angry populace pressed relentlessly toward the castle. Momentarily Tor's men stood firm like a scarlet island in a flood, and watched the crowd flow past them.

Then they lowered their instruments, and above the pulsating uproar came the triumphant sound of trumpets.

Forzon found himself alone in the room. This was the moment Team B had awaited for four hundred years, the crisis it was superbly prepared to exploit. Already Leblanc had pushed out into the square to exhort the crowd. Directly below Forzon's window Joe was waving his arms wildly and shouting at the top of his voice, but none of his words reached Forzon. So deafening had the clamor become that even the trumpets were blotted out. Tor's men lowered their instruments and dazedly stood watching the surging crowd.

Across the square the angry vanguard had filled the castle's courtyard. Forzon doubted that it could force the sturdy inner doors with the sheer weight of numbers, but that was Leblanc's problem. He had the uprising he wanted; he would know what to do with it. Forzon turned, found Ann standing beside him. Her lips moved, but he could not hear her. He shook his head, and they stood smiling at each other for a moment, and then he swept her into his arms.

Suddenly a shadow swooped across the square, and in that instant the crowd halted in its tracks and went silent, with thousands of pale faces turned upward.

Forzon released Ann, and they stood at the window gazing dumbfoundedly at the hushed crowd.

The shadow returned. A plane drifted slowly over the square at low altitude, one of the noiseless planes IPR maintained for its Kurr contacts. Not even a muffled purr reached Forzon as it floated overhead. A moment later it was back, climbing slowly. It circled above the castle, and then it dove.

The crowd fled in pandemonium. A solid mass of people that had been hours in gathering vanished in minutes. Those already in the castle's courtyard had been too intent on smashing the doors to notice the plane, but they sensed the sudden failing of support from the square, wavered, and were driven back through the gate by the ruffs. Then the plane dove again, and they made a frenzied rush for the safety of Kurr's narrow streets. The ruffs were as panic-stricken as the citizens; they fled headlong toward the castle. With stunning abruptness the square was deserted, except for those who had stumbled in their flight. They lay motionless, and no one came back for them.

The plane continued to circle and dive, and long after the square had emptied it could be seen cruising over the city and dipping down to pursue the Kurrians all the way to their own doors. Finally it shot upward, waggled its wings, and flew away.

Leblanc came in, breathless, his clothing torn, a nasty bruise disfiguring his face. 'Wheeler!' he panted. 'Either he's at the castle or he has someone there.' He paused for breath. 'Wheeler—'

'Did the trumpeters get away all right?' Forzon asked.

'I suppose so. Wheeler—'

'Is that all IPR cares about *people*?' Forzon snapped. 'Pieces you move about and discard once a play is made? You may need those trumpeters again!'

Leblanc said meekly, 'Of course we care. I sent someone to see if they're all right. But Wheeler—' His voice broke.

Others had arrived – Joe, Hance Ultman, Sev Rawner.

161

All had suffered serious cuts and bruises, but they hadn't yet noticed them. They wore the stunned expression of men who had just seen a world come to an end.

The IPR world. After four centuries of superbly skilled concealment, a treacherous officer had abruptly and irrevocably betrayed IPR's presence, in daylight, over the capital city of Kurr, before the shocked eyes of the entire population.

'Sorry,' Forzon said. 'I spoke without thinking. Trumpets can't help you now. Kurr is beyond help. No revolution could succeed here while the king has Wheeler backing him with planes.'

SIXTEEN

Night fell on a dead city.

Hance Ultman, delegated to make a cursory reconnaissance, met no one in the dark streets and failed to find a single tavern torch burning. The city gates were unmanned. Houses were unlighted. Except in the king's castle, where the upper stories blazed with light, the citizens of Kurra huddled trembling in darkness.

A few members of Team B gathered in their subcellar and methodically went about the business of writing reports and comparing observations, but not even this display of iron discipline could disguise the fact that they were, all of them, in a state of shock.

'What about the trumpeters?' Forzon asked.

'They're all right,' Leblanc said. 'A few bruises, a few dented instruments, nothing serious. Any message for them?'

'Tell Tor to keep playing.'

'King Rovva is no fool, as I may have mentioned. He isn't likely to make the same mistake twice. He'll let the trumpeters play.'

162

'I'm afraid you're right,' Forzon said.

'I've never heard of a revolution fizzling out so quickly, but then – I've never heard of treason on the part of an IPR Bureau officer, either. If you have anything else up your sleeve you'd better pull it out before what we gained is a total loss.'

Forzon, with all eyes fixed upon him expectantly, could only shrug and say again, 'Tell Tor to keep playing.'

Rural vendors who had not been in Kurr the previous day passed through the unmanned gates at dawn and set up in the market places – and found no customers. But as the sun rose higher and the huge Bird of Evil with the ugly, swift shadow came no more, people gradually nerved themselves to creep from their homes. They did not congregate in the open, but in the tunneled streets and in the shops they gathered timorously to discuss this phenomenon. The vendors moved their wares from the open markets back under the protective flares of the buildings, and the citizens hastily bought what they needed with very little haggling.

At midday groups of trumpeters marched into the market places. As they sounded defiant blasts they warily searched the sky for the Bird of Evil and the approaching streets for ruffs. They did not play well; neither did they attract the crowds they were accustomed to.

Leblanc told Forzon for the tenth time, 'If you have anything else up your sleeve—'

'Get your communications working again,' Forzon said.

'We wouldn't dare to use them. We'd never know when Wheeler was listening.'

'That plane's timely arrival couldn't have been an accident. Wheeler must be doing some communicating himself. How about listening in on him?'

Leblanc clapped his hands to his forehead and hurried off muttering to himself.

Forzon found Joe Sornel placidly sipping wine while watching the trumpeters perform in the empty market place, and added another item to the list of essential attributes for IPR agents: the ability to relax.

'I almost forgot Coordinator Rastadt,' Forzon said. 'How is he?'

'Still delirious. We had to put him in a soundproofed room. He wakes up screaming about a black box.'

'He would. I don't suppose he knows anything that would be helpful to us, but I'd like to talk with him as soon as he's able.'

'I'll tell Ann,' Joe promised. 'She's looking after him. Anything else?'

'Tell her—' Forzon paused. 'Never mind.'

Joe grinned sympathetically. 'Dames! Say, that was a real good revolution you had going there. I never thought to see one in Kurr. We've talked about it, and we still don't understand how you brought it off.'

'See if you can understand how I can bring it off again.'

Joe shook his head good naturedly. 'It sure was fun while it lasted. I'll go see Ann.'

Leaving the room he almost collided with Leblanc, who stepped around him, seated himself with exaggerated deliberation, and asked, 'Ready for a surprise?'

'I've had very little else since I landed here,' Forzon said.

'Wheeler wants to talk with you.'

'Really? On the radio?'

'In person. He was broadcasting an automatic blanket signal, wanting you to call him on channel one. So I called on channel one, got his communications man, and Wheeler was on within a minute. He wants a personal interview with you.'

'Confident, isn't he? Or should the word be "audacious"?'

'I kept him on long enough to get a couple of readings. He's at the castle – not that it's any surprise. I told him you weren't immediately available, but I'd give you his message when you came in. He's waiting for your answer. He in-

164

sists that it be no later than tonight. If that sounds like an ultimatum, he probably thinks that it is one.'

'Where does he want to see me?'

'He was politely noncommittal, except that he'll guarantee your safety at the meeting place and coming and going.'

'His word of honor?' Forzon asked with a grin.

Leblanc nodded grimly. 'I was hoping you'd see it that way. Now I can tell him what I think of him.'

'Wait. I'd like to know what he wants, but not badly enough to stick my hands into a black box to find out. Couldn't we guarantee *his* safety?'

'Yes—'

'Let's do it that way. He'll have to rely on our word of honor, because King Rovva doesn't make coins small enough to evaluate his. Tell him that.'

Leblanc went to deliver the message frowning skeptically and returned with a broad smile on his face. 'He really does want to see you.'

'You made the arrangements?'

Leblanc nodded. 'For tonight. And I told him that if a single ruff is sighted the guarantee is off.'

'That's hardly fair,' Forzon observed. 'He can't be responsible for all of the king's ruffs.'

'Oh, no? He didn't even take time to blink before he accepted. Either King Rovva approves of this, or Wheeler has more influence with him than I would have thought possible. Now if you'll excuse me – if this is a trap I want to make certain that it closes the right way.'

Watching from a window slit, Forzon saw Wheeler saunter casually across the castle square and enter a side street. The assistant coordinator still looked the clown – looked so grotesquely miscostumed in Kurrian dress that if Forzon hadn't known better he could have believed that the man was deliberately made up to get laughs. Hance Ultman emerged from a doorway to fall into step with him, and the two of them took the first turning and disappeared.

Leblanc was scrutinizing the passersby with binoculars. 'It looks all right,' he announced, 'but we'll carry out the program anyway. As soon as it's dark they'll blindfold him and take him for a tour of Kurra, with a few tunnels thrown in. Then they'll bring him back here. It's probably an unnecessary precaution, but maybe they'll be able to walk some of the arrogance out of him.'

It was nearly midnight when Wheeler finally arrived, escorted by Ultman and Joe Sornel. Forzon suspected them of maliciously giving him a longer walk than Leblanc had intended. Wheeler, perspiring profusely, ripped off his blindfold and demanded, 'Was that necessary?'

'Kurr is a very dangerous place these days,' Joe said cheerfully. 'We can't be too careful.'

Wheeler nodded coolly at Leblanc and then exclaimed, 'Ah! Forzon!' He strode forward with hand outstretched; Forzon ignored it.

'You wanted to talk with me,' Forzon said. 'Talk.'

'Alone,' Wheeler said.

'Did you search him?' Leblanc asked.

'We put him through a sieve,' Joe said with a grin.

'All right, Wheeler. But I'm not trusting you alone with the supervisor. We'll use the big room downstairs. You can talk as confidentially as you like in the far corner, but the rest of us will be there watching.'

Wheeler said slyly, 'That isn't very flattering to you, Supervisor.'

'Nor to you.'

Wheeler grinned mournfully. 'I like you, Forzon. I've liked you from the beginning.'

'What about the coordinator – do you like him, too?'

'Rastadt is a cowardly bully,' Wheeler said matter-of-factly. 'I hate his guts.'

'At least no one can accuse you of partiality in your treason. You're as willing to betray a person you like as one you dislike. Let's get this over with.'

They seated themselves on the far side of the dwelling's

166

main room, Wheeler looking about suspiciously. 'How do I know Leblanc hasn't netted this place?' he demanded.

'Why would he bother?' Forzon asked. 'As soon as you leave I can tell him everything you said.'

'But will you? That's what he'll be asking himself. Will you tell him – *everything*? So this place may be netted.'

Forzon called across the room to Leblanc, who sat watchfully near the door with Sornel and Ultman. 'Wheeler thinks this place may be netted.'

Leblanc snarled an angry denial. Wheeler said softly, 'I raise the question for your benefit, Supervisor. You may not want to tell him everything.'

'In spite of some excellent instruction from King Rovva in the art of being patient, I find that I'm getting less patient all the time. You have something to say to me? Say it.'

He was studying Wheeler narrowly, searching for the tragic clown that he remembered; but this man had changed, or perhaps Forzon was finally reading his character correctly. Behind the clown mask was a sinister craftiness that repelled. The perennial underling, the man destined to spend his life as an assistant because no one would take him seriously, had suddenly emerged on top and was exulting in it.

'I'll make you a proposition,' he said confidently. 'I'll trade the IPR base for Kurr.'

Forzon gawked at him.

'As you pull Team B out of Kurr,' Wheeler went on, 'I'll move the base personnel to Kurr – those who want to come. Any of Team B who want to join me will be welcome. When everyone who wants to leave this planet is at base, and everyone who wants to stay is in Kurr, you can notify Supreme Headquarters that the planet is blown and request evacuation.'

'And leave you in Kurr? Don't be ridiculous. Haven't you given any thought to what Supreme Headquarters will do to you?'

Wheeler laughed. 'A great deal of thought. Supreme

Headquarters will do – nothing! By that time I'll be king of Kurr, and the IPR Bureau's regulations won't let it interfere directly with a ruling monarch. Any action would have to be taken by the people, and IPR can't stay around to foment action because the planet is blown. If it did anything at all it would be making a bad situation worse. So it'll evacuate, and leave Gurnil to me.'

Forzon said dazedly, 'Let me get this straight. You deliberately blew the planet so IPR would have to leave, and you think that you—'

'I *know*!' Wheeler exulted. 'I've been planning this for years. Sorry you had to get mixed up in it, but you arrived at a critical moment and I couldn't take a chance on your ruining everything. As it turned out you've given me a big boost – put me a full year ahead of schedule. I'll take over Kurr in a matter of days.'

'How did I give you a boost?' Forzon demanded.

'That uprising you staged. It scared King Rovva witless. Gave me a chance to intervene dramatically, and now he's completely dependent on me. Won't do a thing without consulting me. How the devil did you manage it?'

'Cultural Survey has its own secrets.'

'I'm almost inclined to believe you. It would have been interesting to see how far it would go, but I couldn't let it get out of control. Taking over a totalitarian government is relatively simple: if the proper ground work is done and enough key officials are won over, one simply displaces the king and everything proceeds exactly as before. But if the people were to overthrow the king and set up some other form of government I might be stymied indefinitely. So I had to stop it.'

'Then you actually think you can become king of Kurr, and Supreme Headquarters—'

'Look,' Wheeler said earnestly. 'You saw the IPR handbook. You've surely grasped enough of its sacred principles to understand that it can't violate a single one of them without destroying the whole foundation of its existence. If the natives even suspect the presence of IPR it has to withdraw. In order to take action against me and the IPR personnel loyal to me it would have to stage an all-out military campaign, and the effect on the natives would be so cataclysmic that it might never be forgotten. For all practical purposes IPR would lose Gurnil permanently. It doesn't dare risk that, so it'll ignore me and evacuate the planet.'

'And what do you gain?' Forzon asked bluntly.

'A world!' Wheeler said, his eyes shining. 'After spending my life eating dirt for incompetent coordinators and watching them honored and promoted for my work, I'll be absolute master of a world. As soon as I have Kurr firmly in hand I'll take Larnor. I have enough technological equipment for a fair-sized military invasion, but that shouldn't be necessary. With my IPR knowhow, and working without IPR's silly restrictions, I won't have any difficulty in subverting the country. And once this world is mine I'll take steps to keep it that way. I'll educate my people to be on the lookout for IPR snoops. If I do the job properly – and I know how to do it properly – I can render Gurnil immune to IPR for generations and preserve the throne for my descendants.'

'Descendants?'

Wheeler grinned. 'There are a number of attractive girls at base who wouldn't mind being queen. I'll have plenty of descendants. Look. There's a place for you here, too. I'll need capable administrators for both continents. You seem to understand these people. Stay with me, and I'll make you Governor-General of Kurr.'

'No.'

'How about the trade, then – Kurr for the IPR base.'

'No. You've given me added incentive to keep Team B here and bring about that revolution before you can take over.'

'You haven't time.'

'It doesn't take long. You don't realize how quickly I produced the other one once I figured out how to do it. If I'm too late to overthrow King Rovva I can lead a revolt against you just as easily and with a great deal more satisfaction. In a sense the king is a victim of circumstances, but I can easily convince myself that you've asked for it.'

'I'm not quite as culturally naive as you think,' Wheeler snapped. 'I know it was those stupid trumpet players that caused the uprising. I don't understand how or why, but I know that they did it.'

'Right. And I'll tell you why because there's nothing you or anyone else can do about that. The people of Kurr have an unusual musical sensitivity, and trumpet music arouses their martial instincts.'

'I can do something about it.'

'You can't do anything about their musical sensitivity. Actually, they're sensitive to all forms of beauty and they have a natural revulsion for ugliness. That's why I predict a dire end for you if you become king.'

Wheeler regarded him blankly. 'Dire – why?'

'Because you aren't beautiful.' Forzon turned wearily. 'Paul, I'm tired of looking at his unbeautiful face. As supervising coordinator do I have the power of promotion and demotion on this planet?'

'Subject to review by higher headquarters,' Leblanc said.

'Put an official entry in Team B's files. Wheeler is demoted to the lowest IPR rank available, cited for insubordination or treason or whatever IPR regulations provide for, and ordered confined to his quarters at base.'

Wheeler guffawed merrily.

'Get him out of here,' Forzon said.

Joe Sornel and Hance Ultman blindfolded Wheeler and marched him off into the night. Leblanc crossed the room and took a chair near Forzon.

'IPR has a choice mess on its hands,' Forzon observed.

'I heard every word.'

'You lied!'

Leblanc shook his head. 'There are ways of eavesdropping without netting a place. This room has exceptional

170

acoustics, and you two weren't exactly whispering. But you're right. This is undoubtedly the worst mess in IPR Bureau history.'

'At least now we know what the mess is about.'

'Obviously Wheeler was a very good assistant coordinator,' Leblanc said thoughtfully. 'A coordinator like Rastadt would come to be wholly dependent on him, so Wheeler has been commanding Gurnil for years, in Rastadt's name. His itch to be a big-shot led him to meddle rashly in Kurr, and in the blowup that followed he and a number of others were captured by the ruffs. We thought he escaped and rescued the others through his own brilliance, but he probably bought the king off by pretending to turn informer – though he never told him more than suited his own purpose. He never revealed the full extent of Team B's strength and entrenchment until he had to, when he wanted Team B eliminated, and then it so roiled His Majesty that he lost his temper and had Tor's arm severed in public.'

'He's a very good actor,' Forzon observed. 'At least – he certainly put on a good act for me. I walked into that Kurrian trap without a ghost of a suspicion. So did Rastadt.'

'We're all good actors,' Leblanc said dryly. 'The rest of us use our talents for loftier purposes. Wheeler is also resourceful. And adaptive. Consider how he reacted when he learned that a supervising coordinator had been appointed for this planet: he simply suppressed your orders and awaited developments. When you arrived without orders he immediately forged a set that would enable him to get rid of you and at the same time advance his relationship with King Rovva.'

'And when I staged a revolution he used it to get back into the king's favor.'

'Right.'

'At least we know that he hasn't reported the planet blown. We still have some time. The question is, time to do what?'

'Shall we leave now? We're writing this house off permanently, just in case Wheeler managed to have himself followed. As for the rest – you're the ranking officer on Gurnil. The mess isn't of your making, but it's your responsibility. Let me know when you decide what you want done.'

They followed a circuitous route back to the dwelling by the south market. It was dawn when they arrived; the city gates had opened, and carts and wagons loaded with produce were creaking through the streets. Leblanc called for breakfast, and a few minutes later Ann came in to serve it.

'That's a waste of talent,' Forzon observed, when she had left them. 'Isn't it about time you gave her something else to do?'

'Yes,' Leblanc agreed. 'A waste of talent. Can you suggest something more suitable?'

Forzon did not answer.

'How are the hands?'

'Healing. I don't really need the bandages.'

'Then remove them. They're rather conspicuous.'

He stripped them away himself, and pronounced Forzon fit enough so long as he avoided sliding down ropes in the immediate future. They finished eating; Forzon sought out Ann, to see if Rastadt was able to talk.

'He seems to be much better,' she said. 'He had a restful night, but he may be still asleep. I'll look.'

She tiptoed into Rastadt's room and darted out again a moment later, in headlong flight for the stairway. Forzon looked in at the open door; the room was empty. He hurried after her.

She was babbling incoherently to Leblanc. 'The coordinator—'

'What about him?' Leblanc demanded.

'He's gone!'

SEVENTEEN

Leblanc sounded the alarm; he snapped a word of explanation and the available agents headed for the streets, Forzon among them.

Leblanc caught Forzon at the door. 'This is no job for you!' he snarled. He brushed past him and hurried away, dodging through the market traffic.

Forzon found Ann at the window slits, disconsolately searching the market with binoculars. 'I thought he was having a quiet night,' she said brokenly. 'So I went to sleep.'

'It's no one's fault,' Forzon said. 'Rather, it's our fault – Leblanc's and mine. We should have given him a full-time nurse instead of having people with other duties look after him in their spare time. I think Leblanc has made another mistake in sending everyone dashing to look for him. That kind of search is no search at all. Where would he go?'

She shook her head.

'He'd picked up enough language during his captivity to be able to communicate with his guards,' Forzon mused, 'and since he's an IPR veteran, being adrift in a strange society won't be a novelty to him. He may not be as helpless as one might think. How was he dressed?'

'Just in an underrobe.'

'A no-handed man in an underrobe. He shouldn't be difficult to find if the ruffs don't find him first. No-handed men must be a very rare sight in Kurra.'

'A one-handed man is a rare sight. The only ones people see are headed out of the city – fast. Except—'

They stared at each other. 'The trumpeters!' Forzon breathed.

173

'He'd probably be taken for a one-handed man,' Ann said, 'and if he's still incoherent people would think he's a trumpeter who's ill or intoxicated.'

'And they'd take him to the other trumpeters?'

'Perhaps. They'd certainly look after him. Trumpeters are the heroes of the moment.'

'Do you know where they're staying?'

She nodded.

'Let's go!'

'Wait!' she said.

She was back in a moment, miraculously transformed into a middle-aged Kurrian woman. It was not a miracle that Forzon approved of, though he grudgingly conceded its necessity. She gave him a hooded cloak, and they started out.

On this second day after the awesome visit of the Bird of Evil, life in Kurra seemed to have returned to normal. Streets were filled with pedestrians, and the creaking of a steady procession of carts and wagons rent the air. They struggled briefly against the current of market-bound traffic, and then Ann turned aside and led him on a zigzag route through narrow, less traveled side streets.

They emerged on another main thoroughfare, and she pointed out, far up ahead of them, the dwelling where the trumpeters were staying. They hurried toward it.

Suddenly she gripped his arm. 'Look the other way!'

They strolled briskly past the building as far as the first intersection and turned a corner. 'What's the matter?' he demanded.

'Didn't you notice? The street's full of ruffs. One of them was looking you over suspiciously.'

'Did I do something wrong?'

'You dropped your hood. He may remember your face from those portraits that were circulated.'

'I see. Then I'd better stay out of sight. You'll have to go alone.'

'Paul would skin me if I left you here. Anyway, there's

a more immediate problem. Why is the street by the trumpeters' dwelling filled with ruffs?'

They turned back and slowly made their way across the thoroughfare, directing cautious glances at the building while they dodged traffic. A wagon was parked there, its *esg* stomping impatiently, and as they gained the far side four men emerged with a long bundle of cloth, which they heaved into the wagon. Behind them two men struggled with a second bundle. The cloth was heavy; the four had handled it without difficulty, but the two staggered under its weight until others hurried to assist them.

Forzon and Ann walked on a short distance and then halted to look at each other blankly. 'What is it?' Forzon asked.

'I don't know.'

'The shape is very suggestive. So is the weight. Are you thinking what I'm thinking?'

'Yes. The ruffs have taken over, and they're going to haul off the trumpeters a few at a time, disguised as bundles of cloth.'

Forzon hurried her back toward the intersection.

'The two of us can't stop them,' she protested. 'We'll have to tell Paul – get help—'

'We don't even know where he is. Come on!'

At the corner they hesitated. A second wagon creaked to a stop behind the first and stood waiting; ruffs were staggering forth with another bundle, and Forzon, watching it closely, thought he detected movement within it. The throngs of pedestrians were paying no attention. Wagons loading or unloading – these were commonplace sights on the streets of Kurra.

Forzon stopped a young man, pointed, shouted into his ear, 'They're taking the trumpeters!'

The youth whirled, stared incredulously. The ruffs heaved their bundle, the *esg* lurched into motion, the wagon moved off.

Forzon stopped another passerby. 'They're taking the

trumpeters!' he shouted. 'In that wagon – they're taking the trumpeters!'

'Trumpeters!' the young man shrieked.

'Trumpeters!' Forzon shouted. 'In the wagon – trumpeters!' Like the instruments, the word was alien to Kurr. Forzon had absently used it at the one-handed village instead of thinking up a native expression. Tor's men brought it to Kurra, and the Kurrians had embraced it along with the music.

On this day it was a magic word. It halted all who heard it. *Trumpeters? Where?* Traffic backed up behind Forzon and overflowed into the street. Passersby veered out to go around, heard the word *trumpeters*, and came to a stop. As the plodding *esg* approached the corner it was brought to a snorting halt by a solid barricade of pedestrians. The word leaped along the street, creating other barricades, and in an instant all traffic came to a standstill.

Into the strange hush that followed, Forzon shouted at the top of his voice. 'They're taking the trumpeters! They're in that wagon, in bundles of cloth! The king is taking them!'

'The king is taking the trumpeters!' Ann shouted.

Forzon began another shout. 'The trumpeters—'

A cloth flipped over his head and jerked tight. Strong arms pinioned his arms and legs, and he was lifted, struggling futilely and roaring muffled protests into the gagging, blindfolding cloth, and carried away. Moments later, securely bound, he was thrown into a wagon. The wagon moved off, its creaking drowning out the upwelling of shouts that he heard behind him. He did not even know that they had taken Ann, too, until long afterward, when the castle gate clanged shut behind them and the cloth was removed.

'Now I've done it,' he said despondently.

'Hush! It had to be done.'

'I didn't have to bring you into it. I should have known that the ruffs would be on the lookout for trouble makers.'

A guard shouted an order, and they waited in silence.

The courtyard thronged with guards, no doubt assembled to take charge of the wagon loads of trumpeters, and they seemed perplexed as to what should be done with two harmless-looking civilians. An officer went to inquire, and then had to return to ask the driver just what offense Forzon and Ann were supposed to have committed.

Finally they were hurried through the castle's taper-lit corridors and up the steep ramps to the audience chamber. Forzon had the disgusted feeling of never having been away. The startled door guards knew him, and rushed the two of them the length of the long room to the high dais, where two men sat waiting. One of them, Gasq, leered at Forzon in triumphant recognition.

The other was Wheeler.

'You fool!' he said in Galactic. 'You should have known enough to stay off the streets. You're of no use to me now. No use at all. As for you—' His scowl vanished. 'Ann, isn't it? This is an unexpected pleasure. I hadn't counted on your brightening my kingdom.'

'Don't count on it now,' she snapped.

'But I think you will,' he said complaisantly. 'I won't try to save Forzon. King Rovva is angry, besides which he is scared stiff, and he must be propitiated. He can have Forzon. But not you. That'd be wasteful.' Gasq began to mutter complainingly, and Wheeler switched to Kurrian. 'We have no secrets from you, friend Gasq,' he protested. 'It's just that we are more comfortable speaking our own language. You remember Supervisor Forzon, don't you? He *would* play in the streets and meddle in things that don't concern him, so you have him back. The woman was an innocent bystander, I'm sure. We must speak sternly to the men who brought her. Well – no. I wouldn't turn her loose. Not just yet.' He laughed. 'I may find a use for her. What is it now?'

Gasq leaped to his feet and strode to the window slits. 'They're back!' he gasped.

Wheeler went to join him. He stood looking out for a

moment, and then he shrugged and said lightly, 'They have shorter memories than I'd supposed.'

Forzon nudged Ann, and the two of them walked over to the window slits. The guards made no objection. They followed along and peered out curiously.

Far across the square the streets thronged with people. Watching them, Forzon reflected that there must be many kinds of revolution: the explosion, the tidal wave – this one flowed with the slow relentlessness of a rising tide. So deliberate was their advance that the people scarcely seemed to be moving.

But it was a revolution. The previous affair had been an impromptu gathering that accidentally turned into an uprising. This crowd marched with *purpose*. The brimming streets and byways debouched a solid mass of Kurrians into the castle square – and remained brimming. The tide edged forward, and no sober-minded person watching it could have doubted that it would continue to move, strongly and inevitably, until it lapped at its intended highwater mark – be that the castle roof or somewhere beyond the Kurrian moon.

As the crowd came closer uneven currents of movement could be seen within it. It put out bold, exploratory tongues and made sudden surges to overtake them. The silence that Forzon had thought curious when he watched from across the square now seemed, with the crowd advancing toward him, fraught with menace. There were fewer women than before, and – the most menacing of all – no children looking on.

'*What do they want?*'

King Rovva had entered unnoticed. One glance at the square, and he recoiled. In terror? Anger? Bewilderment? Forzon was unsure. The guards, Gasq, Wheeler performed the ceremonial bow, and the king shouted again, 'What do they want?'

As if to answer, someone in the crowd called a word.

178

'Trumpeters!' Others took it up, and soon it crashed and resounded about the square. Not shouted. *Snarled*.

'Where are the trumpeters?' the king demanded.

Gasq's glance sent a guard scurrying; he returned to blankly gesture a negative.

'Turn them loose!' the king ordered.

'They aren't here!' Gasq protested weakly.

'Weren't they to be brought here?'

'Yes—'

'Where are they?'

No one knew. The artfully contrived abduction of the trumpeters had foundered somewhere on the streets of Kurra. Forzon flashed a sideglance at Ann and caught her suppressing a smile. Rumor had turned the attempted abduction into a fact, and the citizens had instantly marched on the castle to force the release of trumpeters the king did not have.

The king turned accusingly on Wheeler. 'You said they wouldn't come again!'

Wheeler shrugged. 'That I did not. I said they *would* come if you didn't do something about those stupid trumpeters. Obviously your servants blundered the job, and this is the result. Relax. I'll take care of it. And the next time you want something done ask me first.'

He strode away. The crowd continued to snarl. *'Trumpeters!'*

Ann clutched Forzon's arm. Immediately below them a man had been hoisted onto shoulders.

Rastadt.

Somewhere he had acquired a long Kurrian shirt, which he wore over his underrobe. The flapping collar hung free, and he waved his pathetic stubs of arms in defiance. Probably he was shouting, but the angry chant blotted out all other sounds.

Ann nudged Forzon again. The king had seen Rastadt. He reeled backward like one suddenly confronted with an

179

avenging angel and finally took refuge in a chair high up on the dais.

For the first time he noticed Forzon. 'Come here,' he called. It sounded more like a plea than an order. Forzon went, trailing guards, and dutifully performed the bow. 'You gave them the trumpets. Why?'

'They are only a harmless diversion, Excellency,' Forzon said. 'The people in the one-hand villages were gravely in need of one.'

'Harmless!' the king croaked. He gestured at the window slits. 'Can *you* make them leave?'

'No, Excellency. They want the trumpeters.'

'They aren't here!'

'You conspired to bring them here,' Forzon said boldly. 'Your guilt is none the less in the eyes of your people for having failed.'

'The great Bird will chase them away,' the king muttered. He dismissed Forzon with a gesture, and Forzon bowed again and rejoined Ann.

'Wheeler went to send an S.O.S. for the plane,' he said. 'I know.'

They watched and waited, stooping low to search the skies for the plane.

Wheeler returned. The king leaped to his feet and blurted, 'When is it coming?'

'There'll be a bit of a delay,' Wheeler said.

'Delay!'

'Relax,' Wheeler said with a grin. 'Everything is under control. *I'm* here. But what I can't understand,' he went on, 'is why they aren't afraid. Two days ago the great Bird scared them witless. You, Forzon. You claim to understand the people of Kurr. Why aren't they afraid? Don't they realize that a demonstration like this is likely to bring the Bird back again?'

The king said eagerly, 'Yes, yes – why aren't they afraid?'

Forzon bowed. 'It has been two days, Excellency. The people have had time to think, and they may have thought

180

that the Bird of Evil, terrifying as it seemed, actually did no harm. Citizens were injured and a few of them killed, but that wasn't the Bird's doing. The other birds of Kurr don't harm people. Why should this one?'

He went on thoughtfully, 'I have wondered why they called it that –*Bird of Evil*. Surely they know that it is the king's Bird, and yet – a thing of evil should not derive from the king. Perhaps this is one reason they are so angry, and if the Bird comes again they will become still angrier.'

'Become . . . angrier?' the king muttered.

Wheeler laughed. 'If that's true, which I doubt, you've no cause for worry. The Bird isn't coming.'

'Not . . . coming?'

'Stupid pilot went to base last night to refuel. He's on his way back now, but he won't be here for a couple of hours – too late to be of any use. Maybe it's just as well. If you're right about the people thinking that the Bird doesn't harm them, it's time they had something to think about that does.' He flashed a pair of stun-guns, pocketed them again. 'I'm going down by the gate to bring this nonsense to a fast stop.'

He turned away.

'Wait!' the king shrieked.

He had lost weight in the past few days. His jowls sagged, his face was flabby with wrinkles. Now he had lost his poise and dignity as well. He sprang erect, his sunken eyes wildly staring. 'You!' He pointed a trembling finger at Wheeler. 'You summoned the Bird that my people now call the king's evil!'

'And saved your fat neck with it,' Wheeler said agreeably.

'You said the trumpeters could be captured secretly! You made the plan! You said they must be captured!'

'And so they must. Their trumpets arouse – what was it you said, Forzon? "The martial instincts of the people." They must be done away with, and they would have been,

181

if your men hadn't bungled it. Next time I'll see to it myself. And now—'

The king's sweeping gesture encompassed the festering revolution in the square below. 'You did it!' He snapped a word.

The guards closed on Wheeler.

He snatched at his stun-guns as they seized him, but could not – quite – pull them free. Forzon took a step forward and a dozen guards moved to restrain him. Ann quietly turned away.

Wheeler fought. Whatever else the man was, he had courage. He fought while they stripped away his clothing, he pulled desperately and flailed and scratched with his right arm while they forced his left into position. He made no sound, not even when the sword flashed. Then the pain enraged him, and he snarled obscenities and beat and kicked at the doctor who attempted to work on the spurting stump of his arm. Finally they subdued him and carried him from the room. Pale faced guards cleaned up the mess and scurried away.

The chanting of the crowd had grown louder; the vanguard was making tentative rushes at the gate. The king had collapsed into his chair, where he sat sunken in thought.

'Is there any way to stop them, Forzon?' he called.

Forzon did not realize how shaken he was until he tried to speak. He stammered, 'I don't know of any.'

'What should I do?'

'Lately Your Majesty has had small benefit from the words of advisers,' Forzon said politely. 'You should make this decision yourself.'

The king got to his feet and descended the dais to approach Forzon. 'I must be getting very old,' he said softly. 'I need an enemy to remind me that I am king. You are a strange person. It is difficult to believe that you and Blag are of a kind. The difference, I think, is that you want nothing for yourself. Whom do you serve?'

'Your people, Excellency.'

'And – could you not also serve me?'

'Only insomuch as you are one of your people, Excellency.'

'I – am one – of my people,' the king mused. 'And that which serves my people serves me. We must talk again. Gasq!'

Gasq hurried forward.

'I will leave this place. At once.' He gestured at Forzon and Ann. 'Bring them. Make ready a fast march. I will speak to the Captain of the Guard now. As soon as we're away the gates are to be opened. Let my people satisfy themselves that the trumpeters they seek are not here.'

He swept from the room.

Forzon said bewilderedly, 'Why did he turn on Wheeler and not me?'

'You heard him,' Ann said. 'You want nothing for yourself. Also, you didn't make the mistake of telling him what to do.'

The royal wagons were exquisite models of cabinet work, but they bounced as uncomfortably, and squeaked as loudly, as those with which Ultman had hauled tubers. The caravan left the castle by a rear gate, each wagon pulled by three *esgs* harnessed in single file; to Forzon's amazement the lumbering beasts broke into a trot as they got underway. Ranks of soldiers jogged on either side. Those of the crowd who witnessed their departure watched indifferently; they were too remote to know what was happening at the front of the castle, and seemingly did not realize that the king was in flight.

The wagons sped through deserted streets, passed a city gate where guards crouched at attention, and moved along a dirt road spewing clouds of dust. Ann thought they were headed for the royal preserves, where the king maintained a rural residence and a substantial garrison. He had sent the queen and her young sons there after the first uprising.

The *esgs* could not keep up the brisk pace for long; they

resumed their normal, plodding gait, and the wagons moved slowly through the verdant Kurrian countryside. At midday they reached a village and a cross road. The king passed this way often, and the villagers had seen his royal wagons approaching and dutifully marshalled their hospitality. Food and drink were supplied to those in the wagons, and the perspiring soldiers moved about with jingling coins buying up the village's stock of wine. The king summoned Gasq to his wagon, and the two talked while the remainder of the caravan made a leisurely picnic.

Time passed. Dusty files of king's soldiers came marching up the road from the south and scattered about indolently, awaiting orders. Another, much smaller, group arrived at a forced march from the west.

'He sent out fast messengers,' Ann observed. 'By tomorrow his force will have doubled, and if they give him another week it'll have doubled again.'

When finally the king moved it was only a short distance into the rolling country south of the village. There, on the long ridge of a hill, he positioned his army – not in battle formation, but at rest, in the shade of scattered trees. After a time wagons arrived from the south with drink and provisions, and while his troops refreshed themselves the king went from group to group and spoke his orders.

Moving about under the hot sun he had discarded his royal robes and with them sloughed off a lifetime of indolence. He walked with a vigorous stride, his voice rang with new-found authority, and his eyes were bright and eager.

For all that he seemed sad. He came finally to Ann and Forzon, where they sat in a wagon surrounded by guards. Forzon asked, 'Do you think the people will pursue you?'

'They are pursuing,' the king said. 'They will be here soon. My people.' He gazed impassively at the horizon. 'I sent messengers to tell them the trumpeters are not here – that they are safe in Kurra, or if they are not they will be found and restored their freedom to play. But my people

184

are still pursuing. I gravely fear that before I can forgive them I must defeat them in battle.'

He moved on.

Forzon said, 'It won't be much of a battle. His troops will be armed and well rested and fighting on ground of his choosing. This is a steep hill for an unarmed and thirsty rabble to charge after a long march. I think the king will have an opportunity to exercise his forgiveness.'

Ann made no comment, and Forzon kept to himself his thought that after this day King Rovva might be a better man and a much better king.

They heard the pursuing crowd long before they saw it – heard it as a distant gasping blur of sounds that occasionally spewed up a word: *Trumpeters*! As it topped the crest of the next hill the king shouted his troops into a solid battle line.

'Look!' Ann whispered. 'Rastadt!'

Still carried on shoulders, the coordinator hung poised on the skyline for a moment, and then the crowd began to flow down the hill into the valley. It moved with the same slow determination with which it had advanced across the castle square. The valley filled; the vanguard, with Rastadt carried in the front rank, began the steep climb toward the king's lines, still moving with a calm, measured slowness, still the inevitably advancing tide. Behind it the crowd continued to flow over the hill and down into the valley. Even though the quarry had been sighted there was little chanting. The weary crowd came on, in a hushed movement of thousands.

And if it could keep coming, Forzon thought, it might win. No battle line could halt a moving tide with an ocean behind it. Closer and closer the crowd came, and Forzon and Ann searched the advancing faces for the members of Team B who must be among them and waited breathlessly for the shock of battle.

Everything stopped.

Faces turned upward, hoarse cries arose from both forces,

and a plane plummeted downward, bounced, came to rest a few feet from where the king stood.

Wheeler climbed out, a deathly white specter with the stub of a left arm wrapped in blood-soaked bandages. He staggered toward the king, and as guards leaped to intercept him he steadied himself and performed a bow. The king waved the guards away.

Wheeler gestured with his right hand and pointed. His voice carried to them clearly; he was offering to disperse the crowd.

The king laughed at him.

Standing erect, shoulders squared, head held high, arms upraised, for one awesome moment King Rovva's chunky figure held an aura of majesty. 'My people shall answer to me,' he said. 'And I to them.'

The next moment he was dead. Wheeler's right hand pointed a weapon, there was a flash but no sound, and the king crumpled. Wheeler, his face deeply etched with hatred, turned on Gasq and the little group of advisors, who were petrified with terror. The guards, the soldiers, the vast crowd huddled on the hillside – all seemed smitten with paralysis.

Ann tugged at Forzon's arm. The door creaked faintly when they opened it; no one noticed. They moved unhindered past their guards, through the lines of soldiers, and down the hill. A familiar figure stepped forward to meet them. Hance Ultman. He grinned, gripped their hands, pulled them back into the crowd.

'Bow to your king!' Wheeler roared.

The trembling ministers bowed.

Cackling shrilly, Wheeler turned on the nearest soldiers. 'Bow to your king!' he roared. 'Bow to King Blag!'

The soldiers bowed.

'He's *mad*!' Ann whispered.

'What happened to him?' Ultman asked.

Ann told him, and added, 'He had a radio at the castle. After he lost his arm he must have arranged to meet the plane, and he timed himself to arrive here at the moment the king would need him the most – and the king wouldn't have any part of him.'

'Mad,' Ultman agreed. 'And dangerous.'

Wheeler had stepped past the bowing soldiers. He stood on the crest of the hill peering out over the crowd. 'Go home!' he roared suddenly. 'Your king commands you. Go home!'

Suspenseful minutes passed while he stood glowering at the silent, motionless crowd. Abruptly he turned, spoke a few words to Gasq, and sauntered back to his plane. The plane lifted, floated out over the valley, circled, dove.

The crowd remained motionless, faces uplifted and staring.

The plane circled back, dropping so low that those on the ground could have touched it with upraised hands. Wheeler leaned from a window.

'Stun-gun!' Ann gasped.

The plane floated slowly across the valley, and in its wake people toppled like scythed grain. It turned back to cut another wide swathe. And another.

With a quiet laugh Ultman pushed free of the crowd and knelt, training his own stun-gun on the approaching plane. Wheeler, intent on the swathe he was carving directly below, never saw him. Ultman's gun buzzed; the swathe ended abruptly. The plane accelerated, shooting straight ahead and barely clearing the hill as the king's troops scrambled out of the way. At full speed it nosed down into the next valley and dropped from sight. They heard a distant clap of thunder, saw a narrow plume of smoke rising.

When finally the stunned crowd nerved itself to move forward again, the hill was deserted. The king's soldiers were in full flight.

Ann and Forzon went together to see the smashed plane, and Leblanc found them there, attempting to separate the two bodies from the wreckage. Wheeler and a base pilot, Wheeler still clutching his gun.

'They shouldn't have crashed,' Leblanc said. 'This kind of plane *can't* crash, and when it did they should have ejected safely. But they had to trip the safety circuits in order to fly low enough to use the stun-gun.'

'At least Wheeler died happy,' Forzon said. 'He was King of Kurr for all of five minutes. Are the trumpeters all right?'

Leblanc nodded. 'The crowd released them. Then the rumor spread that the king took them, and naturally I didn't want them spoiling things by marching out to give a concert just when the uprising was getting interesting. I gave Joe the job of keeping them out of sight.' He chuckled. 'He'll never forgive me. We finally have a successful revolution, and he's sitting it out in a cellar. We were worried about you. Tor said a man and woman aroused the people by shouting that the king was taking the trumpeters, but he didn't know what happened to them.'

'Nothing happened to us,' Forzon said, 'and I'll never be the same again.'

A crowd of natives gathered silently about the plane, and a little later Rastadt came, borne on the shoulders of admiring Kurrians. He asked to be put down, and he stood for a long time looking at Wheeler's body.

'I didn't want him dead,' he said finally. 'I wanted to see him at a court martial – wanted to see him squirm.'

'He suffered – a little – as you suffered,' Forzon said.

Rastadt shook his head. 'No. I suffered much for little. Bad judgement – was I really guilty of more than that? Bad judgement and growing old. And I paid.' He waved his stubs of arms. 'Oh, yes. I paid.'

'Wheeler also paid,' Forzon said.

'No. Not enough. It didn't happen a little at a time with him, day after day, with the black box. I didn't want him dead. I wanted to see him squirm.'

Tears streaked his face, and he turned and blindly stumbled away. The Kurrians hurried after him protectively.

Ann had been talking with them, and she said softly, 'The coordinator thinks he did it all himself.'

'Did what?' Leblanc demanded.

'Overthrew the king and accomplished Team B's mission. He came staggering into the square just as the people were marching on the castle. He was weak and half delirious, and they picked him up to keep him from getting hurt. He rode on their shoulders at the head of the crowd, and in time they came to think of him as another symbol of what they were rising against. And he kept looking back and seeing that enormous crowd behind him, and he thought he was leading a revolution. In a sense he was. And now he thinks he did it all himself.'

'Then let him think that,' Forzon said.

Leblanc nodded gravely. 'He'll be retired with honors. When the Interplanetary Relations Bureau can write finis to a four hundred year problem, there's glory enough for all. And now—' He smiled. 'It's a strange feeling to have nothing to do. The king's soldiers and ruffs must be mopped up and controlled, and we may have to give the Kurrians a hand from time to time, and make certain that they don't make the mistake of accepting another king. But right now Kurr belongs to its people. I'm curious to see what they'll do with it.'

EIGHTEEN

Sector Supervisor Jef Forzon and Ann Cory, Gurnil B627, were married at Leblanc's peninsular farm, with Tor and his trumpeters to provide music and all 207 members of Team B in attendance. Deputy-Director Smine, of the Interplanetary Relations Bureau, arrived in time for the ceremony, and as soon as it was over he drew Forzon and Ann aside and signaled Leblanc to join them.

'Sorry to be talking business on such a joyous occasion, Administrator,' he said pompously. 'Ah – did you know that we've promoted you? We have. Supreme Headquarters has been going over your report, and several points seem to require additional explanation. I've been asked to investigate personally. I realize that this is hardly an auspicious moment, but I'm due on Purrok in three days, and if I don't talk to you now—'

'That's quite all right,' Forzon said absently. 'What points require additional explanation?'

He had eyes only for Ann, a beautiful bride with a Kurrian costume in rich, dark hues to set off the gleaming gold in her hair. He was determined that she would never again make herself up as a middle-aged woman – not even when she became middle-aged.

'Frankly, all of them,' Smine said. 'Supreme Headquarters just can't figure out how you used trumpets to bring off a revolution. The music is stunning – even *I* can tell that – but a revolution, now—'

'It really wasn't complicated, sir,' Forzon said. 'We had a people who were profoundly artistic and musical, and a king who'd forgotten he had a conscience.'

Ann was watching him proudly; Leblanc was grinning. The Deputy-Director snapped, 'Leblanc, do *you* understand it?'

'No, sir.'

'Then it's small wonder that Supreme Headquarters is confused. They even had someone in from Cultural Survey to explain it to them, and he couldn't. Perhaps you'd better start at the beginning.'

'I did,' Forzon said. 'We had a uniquely artistic and musical people with a genuine passion for beauty. We had a king who'd forgotten he had a conscience, and you must remember that the king was a typical Kurrian with as much passion for beauty as any of his subjects. That's important.'

'All right,' Smine said dryly. 'I'll remember it. Go on.'

'Well, then. The king's unspeakable cruelties were inflicted on only a few of his people. It rarely happened in his presence, and the screams from the torture chambers weren't heard in the king's apartments. Either way he never saw his victims again. He'd forgotten he had a conscience because his conscience was never tested. And the people were willing to overlook his restricted cruelties as long as he gave them the beauty they wanted. It was only when he attempted to thwart their passion for beauty that they rebelled.'

'I remember that point,' Smine said. 'The woman and the priest's robe. I can't understand it, but I can accept it.'

'All that was needed was something to bring the king's conscience into conflict with the people's passion for beauty, so I gave the one-handed villages the trumpet. The Kurrians were instantly enamored of the music, and why not? A few blurted notes on a radically new musical instrument would have fascinated them, and Tor's trumpeters played superbly. The king was as overwhelmed as his subjects. The day the trumpeters arrived he dismissed everything else from his mind, even the threat posed by Team B, and sat all afternoon at his window listening to the music. *And he didn't realize that the trumpeters were his one-handed victims.* He saw them only from afar, their cloaks hid their mutilated arms, and no one who had access to him would have dared tell him who they were.

'Being a good king who gave his people what both he and they wanted, he ordered a festival to feature the trumpeters. Not until he saw them close by, from his royal box, did he learn that they were one-handed. The realization so confounded him that he sat there like a stone and let them play on and on for hours.

'But once the festival was over he had to do something, and quickly. He'd been so accustomed to having his victims out of sight and memory that he couldn't tolerate the prospect of seeing them everywhere he went, playing music and surrounded by enthusiastic crowds. Inevitably he banned trumpet music and ordered the trumpeters back to their one-hand village.

'That brought his conscience into direct conflict with the national passion for beauty. The music was magnificent, the people saw no harm in it, and just as inevitably they refused to let the trumpeters go. The good king was suddenly no longer good, and the more the people contemplated his past acts in the light of their thwarted passion for trumpet music, the more they saw that they disliked. When the king invoked a sinister Bird of Evil to attack them, their reasoning took the next logical step and they began to regard the king as evil.

'And that's all there was to it: a people with an overwhelming passion for beauty, a king with a neglected conscience, and a great musician to bring the two into conflict. With all of the ingenious connivance that Team B could exercise, of course. Is that explanation enough?'

'Well—' The Deputy-Director scowled thoughtfully. 'What I must have, Administrator, is the underlying principle of the thing. Something in universal terms that would be applicable elsewhere.'

Forzon nodded understandingly. The IPR Bureau wanted a catch phrase that it could put in large, black type in Field Manual 1048K, something like DEMOCRACY IMPOSED FROM WITHOUT, and all the rest.

'Look at it this way,' he said. 'Not even the most unprincipled king can ignore a conscience that starts sounding off on trumpets.'